True Choices

Books by Willow Madison

True Nature

True Beginnings

True Control 4.1

True Control 4.2

we were one once 1

we were one once 2

Existential Angst

the SAYER

True Choices

Willow Madison

Madison, Willow

True Choices (True Series, Book Three)

Front Cover Design by David Colon (www.colonfilm.com); Back Cover Design by XIX (www.thenineteen.net)

This is a work of fiction. Names, characters, places and incidents are either the product of the author's imagination or are used fictitiously, and any resemblance to actual persons, living or dead, business establishments, events or locales is entirely coincidental.

This book is intended for adults only. Spanking and other sexual activities represented in this book are fantasies only, intended for adults. Nothing in the book should be interpreted as advocating any non-consensual spanking activity or the spanking of minors.

www.willowmadisonbooks.com

ISBN-13: 978-0-9963191-3-3
ISBN-10: 0-9963191-3-1

1 Her

The drive back to the house seems shorter. *Maybe because I'm distracted by the rock on my finger.* I giggle to myself, stealing a look at Max, who has his hand in my lap. I put my left hand over his, the ring still shines in the lowering sunshine.

I can't believe all that has happened in such a short time. My head is literally swimming. Oh, my God, I need to stop screaming in my head. I laugh and Max turns his head to smile at me, squeezing my thigh.

We went from the bottom of my betrayal two days ago, to the depths of his anger, to this. We're engaged. *And I'm the luckiest girl in the world. I get to be Mrs. Max Traeger.*

I squeeze his hand and Max smiles again, keeping his eyes on the thick holiday traffic. I know he doesn't want to keep his family waiting. We have plans for an afternoon ride around the lake. Max is very punctual. Being late is a serious pet-peeve.

I've learned about all of his pet-peeves. *Well, rules really*. I swallow. Looking at my beautiful ring, taking up most of my finger, like a large brick, I know that I might as well be honest with myself. I have rules to follow. Being his wife, I will probably have even more rules to follow. And more consequences if I don't.

I shift in my seat. Even with the small pillow Max allowed me, the lowest part of my butt still hurts from when he spanked me two days ago. I shudder just thinking about how angry I made him. I don't ever want to get him that angry again. It took him all night to finally forgive me.

"Lucy, are you cold?" Max saw me shudder and is raising the car windows.

"No. I'm fine." I smile at his attentiveness. He always notices everything. "Thank you."

I'd broken so many of his rules on Saturday, I'm still ashamed. And I tested him, to see if he'd let me get away with acting like I could do as I please around my friends. *I won't make that mistake again*!

I left my phone at his parent's lake house. I didn't want to see all the missed calls and messages from Tracy and Laura. I've been ignoring them since Saturday. I know what they want to say anyway.

I'd misbehaved, *monumentally*, at our company picnic. And they saw Max's angry reaction. They heard me apologize to him and call him Sir. Tracy flipped out. I almost laugh remembering how red her face was; it matched her hair. And Laura...I think she was just more shocked than anything.

I don't want to think about them now, though. Not today. I pull my left hand up again and watch the ring sparkle.

Max laughs at me. "You're going to go blind staring at that."

"You don't think...it's too big?" The ring is very simple. It's a simple platinum band with one simply large diamond that sits horizontally across my finger. Max was very proud to tell me all about picking out the stone and setting himself. He had this made just for me. The engraving says, "Always," just like the watch he gave me.

Max takes my left hand and kisses my palm. This never fails to send little shockwaves down my stomach. He's so tender and gentle. "No. I told my jeweler that I wanted everyone in a fifty-block radius to know you're mine. I think it'll do the job." He winks at me.

We pull into the gravel drive of the house. I'm suddenly very nervous.

We've had the day to ourselves, the most perfect day. I've been able to daydream about our wedding and our life together. But this is reality. We have to tell his parents, his brother. I don't know how they'll react. We've only known each other for such a short time. *Oh, God. I'm going to have to tell my parents and brother.*

I'm starting to feel a little queasy as I watch Max come around to open my door. His smile falters when I'm standing next to him and he sees that I'm not smiling anymore.

He pushes his body into mine against the closed car door. With both hands on the sides of my face, he kisses me and whispers into my ear, "You'll be fine."

He always knows what I'm thinking. He says he loves that I'm so expressive. "What if...what if they don't really want you to marry me?" I know the opinion of his family, especially his dad's, is very important to him.

"Relax," he takes my hand and we walk towards the steps. I try to breathe a little deeper, but feel like I'm choking on my dry throat.

Inside, we can hear laughter coming from the terrace. I follow slowly behind Max through the house and stop at the French doors. I try to stay hidden behind him, but Max won't let me. He steps aside and puts his arm around my shoulder, pushing me forward with him. All three Traegers are staring at us; I look at my feet instead of meeting anyone's eyes.

"Well?" Ron, his dad, speaks first.

"Say hello to your future daughter-in-law." I swallow and jump my eyes up to Max. He's beaming with such happiness and pride that for a second I don't even hear anything else.

Alex, his mom, jumps up from her seat and runs around to us, grabbing me and hugging me to her chest. "Congratulations! We're so excited!" She grabs my hand and says how beautiful the ring is.

Ron stands and shakes Max's hand congratulating him, before turning to me and putting his arms out. I hesitate before squeezing back his embrace. This is the closest I've been to the man. He's only shook my hand before, very formal. It's where Max gets all of his rules and old fashioned ways, from Ron.

He's nearly as tall as Max and I can feel that his back and stomach muscles are strong. He doesn't let go, holding me in a side hug, while Alex continues hugging and kissing Max. "Jake, get up and congratulate your brother and his bride." I jump at the edge in Ron's voice. So like Max's.

I've avoided looking at his brother. He always puts me on edge. This morning wasn't any different. His mix of kindness and something else...like he's looking through me. I hear the chair scrape the deck, but keep my eyes down.

"Congratulations, Max. I'm sure you'll both be very happy." He hugs Max and I steal a look. They are brothers in a mirror, same dark waves, green eyes, tall and muscled. Max's hair is shorter, his eyes lighter, but they could be twins. Only three years apart, Max is older at 35. He loves to mock Jake by calling him "little brother." I drop my eyes again before Jake turns to me.

Ron lets go and I sway a little. I've locked my knees to stop from shaking and held my breath for too long. Jake grabs me in a hug, but doesn't press against me, just holds me up with his strong arms. He kisses my head, tenderly, "You'll make a beautiful bride, Lucy." He lets go when Max stands next to me again.

I finally look at Jake when he sits back down, watching us. His look is almost unreadable, but I can see a hint of something, a little darkness. I turn away and bury my face in Max's chest. I'm sure Jake is thinking about Julia. Our happiness has to hurt in the face of his recent break-up with her.

"So, have you decided any details...?" Ron is sitting back down. Alex has run off towards the kitchen.

I'm surprised when Max answers, "We'll get married next month." He smiles at the stunned look on my face. I glance at Jake but look away just as quick when I see his matching shocked look. "I haven't decided where. One of the LPE places in the city maybe." Max's voice sounds far away to me. I can't grasp that he's discussing our wedding so matter-of-factly. *We haven't discussed any of this.*

Alex is returning with a tray of glasses and an iced bucket of champagne. I remember seeing this on the counter when we walked in. It only just dawns on me that they knew all along that Max was going to propose today. And they knew I'd say yes. "What about having it here...on the lawn?" She sets the tray in front of Ron.

"That's a great idea," Ron is opening the champagne, the pop is soft but I still jump. I feel like I'm watching from a distance. "We could get a tent...do something to make it real nice."

"I'll think about it. I can get one or more of the LPE restaurants to cater, but this might be a little too much of a drive. Could be nice as long as the weather holds up, though." Max holds a chair for me to sit and I'm glad to take it. My knees feel a little shaky still. He keeps talking about which of the restaurants he would most likely use. Since he's a partner in the largest restaurant/bar owner/management group in the city, he can have his choice.

"What do *you* want, Lucy?" Jake is sitting on the other side of the table from me. The dark blue water of Lake

Michigan frames his shoulders and face. He spoke very quietly, but all eyes turn to him, then me.

"I..." I swallow and say in small voice, "I don't know...I...we haven't talked about all that yet..." I shoot my eyes at Max. He hands me a glass of champagne with a wink.

"To my Lucy. To our future." Everyone raises a glass; Jake last. I take a big sip.

Jake downs his and reaches for more. "Take it easy, son. You're driving the boat tonight." Ron says this with that same edge to his deep voice. *Max is so like him.*

I think Jake's going to say something back for a second. Instead, he stops pouring and mumbles, "Yes, Sir."

"And you two better change...it'll probably be a little chillier on the water." Alex is nodding at Max and me.

Max stands up and pulls my chair for me. I take another big gulp before setting my glass down and getting up.

Going up the stairs, I watch how the light catches the ring. It definitely gets attention, just like Max wanted. *No mistaking that I'm taken.* This makes me smile and relax again.

At least his family seemed happy; that went better than I expected. At the top of the stairs, I turn and put my arms around his neck. He's still a little taller than me, but I can easily kiss his forehead. He picks me up around my waist and carries me backwards towards our room, kissing.

"Get changed quickly." He swats my butt, eliciting a small yelp, since it's still sore. "You still have to call your family."

Oh, God. Why did he have to remind me?! "I can do that when we get back..."

His smile changes slightly, a little more crooked, a little frown to his brow. I hurry over to my suitcase and pull out the long dress I brought. Max wouldn't let me bring any pants or shorts. He likes me to look girlie and feminine. I'd rather be wearing jeans and a sweatshirt on the water, but I don't have any choice.

It's the end of summer; the nights are already crisping. The three-quarter sleeve, long cotton dress is the best option I brought. I have a long wool cardigan too. "How's this?" I turn so Max can see me. He's just pulling on a V-neck sweater over his head, the deep olive color compliments his eyes.

He grins, "You look great...but you're still going to freeze. I'll get a scarf and gloves for you from Mom." He starts to leave, but turns at the door and nods with a stern look again towards the dresser, "Your phone's over there."

I walk slowly over to it. I have five missed calls; I don't look to see the details. Ten new text messages that I ignore as well. I pick my parents out of the long list of contacts.

Dad picks up. "Hi, Dad. It's Lucy." I try to put all the happiness I was feeling earlier into my voice again.

"Hey, sweetheart." He pulls his mouth away from the phone a little, "Lizzie! It's Lucy on the phone." Dad hurts my ear yelling into the background for Mom.

Mom picks up another phone loudly. "Hi, sweetie! ...How's your visit going?" She sounds abnormally excited to hear from me.

I take a deep breath and hold it for a second. "I have some news..." My voice sounds extra high to me.

Mom actually squeals in high-pitched excitement, but Dad says calmly, "Let her *tell* us first, Lizzie..."

"Max and I are engaged." I say it slowly, waiting to hear their reaction. They've only met him once.

Mom squeals again and Dad says, "Okay, *now* you can congratulate her."

Mom starts gushing, "Oh that's such great news, Lucy. Congratulations. Max is such a wonderful man*!" I was not expecting this much excitement from her. I know she wants me to be married with a passel of grandkiddies on the way, but...*

"You knew?"

"Max called me yesterday. He's a very formal young man. He asked me for your hand." Dad sounds proud. *Of course Max would ask my dad's permission first. He is very traditional.*

Mom is still giggling on her phone. "He actually used those words, too," she giggles more, "Max didn't say when he was going to ask, but I was hoping we wouldn't have to sit on this news for long! Oh, honey, I'm so happy for you."

"Thanks, Mom."

"Congratulations, sweetheart." Dad sounds like he's tearing up.

"So...details. How did he ask?" Mom's excitement is still running high.

I want to tell her that he didn't ask, technically. He *told* me to say yes. "It was very romantic. He took me to a secluded hilltop above the lake. We had the most perfect picnic and he had the ring wrapped inside a napkin with the silverware. I was completely surprised."

"That is so sweet." Mom still has giggle-fever. Dad only coughs his approval, trying to act like he's not wiping his eyes and nose on his end. His little girl is getting married, after all. "What's the ring look like?"

Huge! "Very pretty, simple...a big solitaire. I'll take a picture with my phone and email it to you."

"Can't wait to see it!" She's obviously moved to be in the same room as Dad; there's an echo now. "Have you two talked about when you want to have the wedding?"

Max has. "We haven't had a chance. Um...but I don't think it's going to be a long engagement, Mom." *Max doesn't like to wait for anything.* "I'll let you know as soon as we decide anything, okay?"

"That sounds fine, sweetheart," Dad answered, "Just give us enough time to work out paying for everything. I have that fund your mom started when you were just a baby...we'll have to see what we need to do to close that out, Lizzie." They're talking to each other more than me.

"Dad? Mom?" They're still talking to each other. "I have to go...Max is waiting for me. ...Mom?"

"Oh. Okay, sweetie. Call us as soon as you can." She kisses into the phone, an echo that pierces my ear. "And send that picture!" She hangs up.

"Congratulations again, sweetheart. Give our best to Max too." Dad hangs up after I say I will.

I put the phone down and hold my forehead. I'm feeling a little fuzzy from all the excitement. This whole holiday weekend has been a rollercoaster of emotions.

"Why didn't you tell them we're getting married next month?" I jump hearing Max's voice from the door.

"I...we...we haven't really talked about anything yet." I'm holding my hand to my chest. I can see the ring sparkling up at me.

"We're getting married next month, Lucy." His face is stern, set.

"I don't think my dad can...I don't think they can afford that, Max." I hear the whine and plea in my voice.

He frowns quizzically at me, like I just said something odd. "*I'm* paying for everything, of course. Your parents don't have to worry about *any* of that. They just need to be here to be a part of our wedding."

"But I don't...I mean...I can't plan a wedding in only a month. I don't even know what all to do." I'm laughing a little. I can't believe I'm pushing for a later date. But the thought of a big wedding in only four short weeks is overwhelming.

"We're getting married next month and that's final." He turns and walks away. I wait before following him downstairs.

I know Max likes being in control, but...but this is our wedding. This is the rest of our lives together. Maybe I'll try to talk to him again when we're back in the city. We really need to make *some* decisions together.

But I know I'm kidding myself. Max doesn't just *like* being in control. Max *is* in control. Period. *That's* final.

2 Him

Lucy's been quiet since her call to her parents. I know this has been a crazy weekend. After everything that happened Saturday, today must seem unreal to her.

I squeeze her hand and she squeezes back, giving me a small smile.

It's just starting to get dark. The dock is a runway of lights up to the house. It is a pretty picture perfect place, with the house all lit up, the sound of waves in the background. *This would make a great spot for our wedding.*

I thought about waiting to propose. I had the ring made last week. After leaving Lucy in the closet Saturday night, after realizing that I could keep her safe from my anger no matter what. I knew I didn't want to wait another moment to see my ring on her finger.

And I won't wait longer than necessary to make her my wife.

I know that's what has her quiet. She's upset about my decision to set the wedding date so soon.

I open the terrace doors and she walks in, hugging her arms around herself. She had a scarf, gloves, and blanket on the boat, but she's still chilled. "I'll get a fire started in the family room."

"Okay. Thanks." She smiles sweetly. She always says please and thank you. It's one of the things I noticed about her the night we met. She stood out then as a sweet girl. *And she'll be my sweet girl always now.*

I tweak her nose. "Get under a blanket." She goes to the sofa nearest the fireplace and wraps a blanket around her huddled body. I get the fire going and sit next to her, wrapping her in my arms to warm her more. She's so tiny, snuggled against my chest.

I'm tempted to just let her have some rest, but we have a few things to discuss and not a lot of time. Jake went with Mom and Dad to pick up dinner, so we could be alone for a little while at least.

"Lucy." She's quick to raise her head to the change in my voice. I only added the slightest hint of my feelings, but she picks up on it so easily. It's one of the things that surprised me most about her in the beginning. I don't have to give her more than a small warning voice or look to get her to change direction quickly. "We need to discuss a few things."

"Yes." She sits up more, but keeps my arm around her, her hands on my leg through the blanket. She likes to keep a physical connection with me when we're together. She takes a quick deep breath and starts talking before I do, "Yes. I don't think it's reasonable to think that we can plan a wedding...the type of wedding that *I'd* want anyway...in only a month." She tries to sound so strong, business-like. I know she's been rehearsing this in her head.

I grin at her, feeling indulgent for the moment, "Oh, is that so?"

She can't make eye contact, instead she concentrates on her hands, fidgeting under the blanket on my leg. "...Yes...I," she pauses for a big swallow, I try not to grin more, "I want a *nice* wedding, a...a...formal wedding...white dress, lots of flowers, my friends..." she pauses, fidgets more, shaking her head a little, "my family all a part of it."

"Of course," I'm really trying not to let the laughter get into my voice. *But she's just so damn cute...trying to look so calm and sound so in control. She knows as well as I do, who's in control here.*

She finally looks at me, tears in her eyes. Her tears are my undoing. I like seeing them. She's even more beautiful lit up this way, her cheeks flushed, her blue eyes bright, my beautiful girl. "I'm serious, Max." She reacts to my darkened brow, "Please..."

"And you shall have *all* of that, Lucy." I touch her cheek and she rubs her face against my hand.

"So...so we can plan for a wedding in maybe six months?" She's using her sweetest, highest voice to try to get me to say yes.

"No. You'll have your dream wedding...*next* month."

"But..."

"Stand up." My indulgence is over.

Lucy freezes at my abrupt change to a deep, commanding voice, one she knows very well. She knows she pushed too far. "If I have to give you an order again, this is going to be a lot worse for you, little girl."

She quickly stands, the blanket getting a little tied up around her, but she manages to get free and not fall over. Her eyes are begging me. "Over my knees."

She hesitates only a second, before getting on my lap. I position her quickly, roughly. Her thin dress won't provide any protection. "You just received a good spanking two days ago, didn't you?"

"Yes, Sir." She's crying already, trying not to by the sounds of her choked words.

"And one of the reasons you were spanked was for questioning me, wasn't it?"

"Yes, Sir." *Her sweet voice, the tears...God, I love her*. I have to stop from smiling, in case she can see me through her thick hair.

"And you're questioning me again, aren't you?" I say this with extra depth, easily hiding my grin.

"Yes, Sir." She's not trying to beg at least; she's learned that lesson.

"I'm going to spank you three times," she shakes at this, "on the part of your bottom I know is still *very* sore, little girl." Her legs lower for a split second, but are quickly raised straight out again. *Good girl.* "Count."

She'd cried out on the boat when Jake went a little too fast over a wave; we all went in the air and she landed hard on her ass. So I know she's even sorer now.

I give her a stinging slap with just my fingers where her ass meets her thighs. She cries out, trying to breathe normally, but she's only able to gasp out, "One."

I spank harder on the same spot, my full hand hitting her this time. Her cry is silent, her body shaking, she again gasps, "Two."

I know her ass is still raw from the belt, from Saturday's spanking. I know that as light as this punishment is it's causing her a great deal of pain. I spank the same spot, just as hard, my full hand making contact again. Her loud cry is drawn in with her breath, and she quickly says, "Three," with the breath going out before she can't speak, her whole body shaking and her breathing only fast hisses.

"You may raise your legs." She lifts her feet to point straight up, just as I've taught her, but not covering her stinging bottom.

I wait for her breathing to slow before letting her stand.

She quickly puts her arms behind her back, "I'm sorry, Sir!"

"Good girl."

"Thank you, Sir." My poor Lucy is raw with emotion and pain. She starts crying and shaking, leaving her hands behind her back, but sobbing openly.

I know she needs this release, so I let her cry for a bit, before pulling her down to sit on my lap and covering her with the blanket again. "You've been through a lot these past few days, little girl." I wipe her tear-stained cheeks and she lowers her head into my neck. Her arms still behind her back, though. *My very good girl.* "You may move your arms, Lucy." She brings her hands to sit in her lap, listless, her emotions calmed and leaving her quiet again.

I take her left hand and play with the ring, making it shine in the firelight. "Do you know what this ring means to me?" She shakes her head and sniffles. "It means that for the rest of your life, you'll *belong* to me." She nods her head, but sniffles more. "That I will always *own* you, Lucy." She nods again.

"And I want you to understand a few things going forward..." I wait until she nods once more. "Questioning me will result in *immediate* punishment," she looks shamefully down, "I don't care *where* we are or *who's* around, I *will* punish you if you talk back to me. Do you understand me, little girl?" I speak slowly, she responds best to this. She answers quietly. "This ring means that you are no longer in control of *anything*." I spell this out as to a child. "So when I tell you that we're getting married next month...that is what we're doing."

I wait for her to think about what I've said so far. "I know you're nervous about that. That you have concerns. I will always try to take into consideration how you feel about something. But you need to understand that in our marriage, I will make all the decisions. That choosing *when* we get married is only the beginning of a long line of choices you no longer have."

She moves slightly in my arms, her head coming up to look at me. "What...what if I really want something...I mean...what if I really don't like a decision that you've made?"

I smile at her, but she doesn't relax. "Then you may *ask* me to reconsider my decision." She thinks about this, her face frowning a little. "But you'll ask respectfully, not talking back, not arguing."

She continues thinking for a moment. I wait to see how she's reacting so far. "So...so if I ask you to reconsider pushing our wedding back a few months, would you?"

Good. Not great, but she's figuring out her limits still. "No. And when I say a decision is final. It is final, that means no more questions, respectful or not. Do you understand me?"

"Yes, Sir."

"Good." I give her a hug and she relaxes a little into my arms, her head back on my chest.

In a very small voice, "So *how* are we going to get married next month then...?"

My very good girl. "I'll need to make a lot of decisions quickly." I laugh at this understatement and Lucy's head moves with my chest.

"I want," she starts off strong, but stops herself and starts again in a more questioning voice, "I'd like my mom to be here to help with picking a dress..."

"Of course, baby." I kiss her head and she relaxes even more. "I was thinking that since your parents are retired, I could fly them out here this week. I want to talk with your dad anyway...explain that I will be paying for everything. I don't want to step on his toes...your still his little girl too...for now."

"I'd like that. Thank you, Max."

"Now, why don't you tell me all the things you've dreamed of for your wedding...?" She gives a big smile and sits up more quickly.

"Well...let's see..." *Uh-oh...this could take a while.* "Big white dress, lots of flowers, tons of them, everywhere, sparkling lights, candles, a big-as....a really big cake," she checks to see if I'm angered by her misstep, but I remain smiling, indulgent again, "dancing, maybe a band or something..."

She's interrupted by the front door. Jake comes in loaded down with three big grocery bags. He stops and stares at us for a second, with the strangest look is on his face. I can't quite make out what he's thinking.

"I thought you were bringing dinner back, not groceries?"

"We were, but Marcello's was closed due to a family emergency. And you know Dad, has to have his spaghetti dinner to end the summer..." Jake rolls his eyes, laughing, the look gone. He heads into the kitchen.

"I should help with the groceries..." Lucy says this as a question though. I told her yesterday that she has to ask my permission before leaving my side. She'll learn that sometimes I only need a questioning look, but for now, I'm proud of her for asking out loud.

"Yes." And she hops up to follow Jake. I head outside to see if there's more to bring in. I didn't get to say everything to Lucy that I wanted, but it's a good start.

3 Her

Phew. No one else is awake. I pad in Max's socks through the kitchen and find the switch for the light above the coffee pot. He went for a run a few minutes ago, so I know I'll have some time to myself.

I have some things to do and I'd rather do them alone.

I look at my phone again. *Start with messages or texts? I'd rather hear how they sound first, I guess.*

"Hey, Lucy. It's Laura...duh right? Are you okay? Are you guys still here? Call me back." I can hear the concern in her voice even with the company party at a distance in the background.

"Luce. Call me back. I'm with Laura by the pool if you're still here." Tracy, minutes after Laura's call.

"Lucy...we're worried about you. Call one of us back!" Tracy again, an hour later.

"Hey...me again...I'm home if you wanna talk...are you still going to Max's parent's tomorrow? If not...well, we could all hang out...please call me!" Laura. She sounded very tired. And very concerned.

"I know Laura just tried to call you too...I'm heading to your place now. Please call me back if you're home and just want to be alone...or if you're not home...or if you wanna come to my place instead...just call me dammit!" Tracy. Sounding very concerned. And still pissed a little.

The last call makes my heart skip though. "Hey, Lucy. It's Rich. Um...I know it's kinda late. I looked for you at the party again, but I don't know if you left early with that guy...I just wanted to check if you're okay...I guess I'll see you tomorrow. Take care." He left the message last night. He thinks I'm going to be in the office today. *Did I give him my number? No...I wouldn't have done that.* He must've looked it up in the company directory. I use my cell for phone interviews sometimes, so it's listed.

I put my phone down after making sure all voicemails are deleted. *Thank God Max didn't hear that one.* I shudder again thinking about how mad Max got when Rich touched my arm a few times at the party. He went ballistic after hearing that I'd gone to lunch with him, even just as a work thing. *If he thought I gave my number to Rich and he was calling me during non-work hours...* I shudder again.

I get a cup of coffee and sit in the family room with the blanket wrapped around me.

Okay. Texts. I take a deep breath before opening the thread from Tracy and Laura. More of the same...concerned pleas to call or text one of them. A last one from Tracy saying that my neighbor's dog won't stop barking at her, so she's leaving. I stare at my phone for a while. It's early, but they're both probably up getting ready for work.

I send a text to Tracy and Laura. "Got your messages. I'm fine. At lake house with Max. Heading home later. I'll call you. xoxo"

"Whatcha doin in the dark?"

I jump, "Shit!" Coffee spills on the blanket and me.

Jake turns on the overhead light, laughing. "You've really gotta watch your language around here, little girl."

I jolt at him saying this. Exactly how Max would've said it, except he doesn't sound so much mad as amused. But I rebound quickly, "And you've gotta stop sneaking up on me!" He scared me yesterday morning the same way, but this time I know Max isn't around to hear me.

Jake gives me that strange, looking through me look again. I want to yell more at him, to curse at him actually, but I don't. I just get up for a towel.

He follows me and heads for the coffeepot. "Get the creamer out." I stop. The fridge is in between us. Jake could just as easily get it himself. He can see that I have a towel in my hand and I'm heading back to the family room.

My mind goes blank. *Is Jake testing me*? Numb, I go to the fridge and hand him the creamer. "Thank you, Lucy." He looks right through me with the same crooked grin that Max wears so often.

I leave with the towel without saying anything.

He follows me though. "Are you texting all your friends the good news?"

I'd left my phone on the arm of the sofa. I pick it up defensively. I have two new texts. "Yes."

"Well I'm sure you're going to be a very busy girl for the next few weeks...if you guys are still planning a wedding for next month that is?"

"Yes. I..." I sit down slowly. That was the other thing I needed to do...start thinking about everything that needs to be done. "Frankly...I'm a little overwhelmed. I've only been to wedding; I've not even stood up in one yet..."

Jake sits on the fireplace stone. "I'm sure Max will make all the big decisions..." He says this into his cup, his eyes looking over the rim at me.

"Yes...I'm sure he will..." I feel we're dangerously close to the edge of a conversation we've already had.

"And this is what you really want, Lucy?"

"Yes. I am sure, Jake." I look him squarely in the eye. "And you really have to stop asking me...it's getting annoying." I stick my tongue out at him, trying to lighten things between us. I don't want to always be on eggshells around him, waiting for him to say something about Max or our relationship.

Jake laughs. It's a big laugh that sets me at ease somewhat. "Okay. I promise...no more questions from me." He laughs a little more. "I've always wanted a little sister...someone I can tease." He sticks his tongue out at me.

He looks so ridiculous that I'm laughing loudly too. He looks so much like is brother, but I could never imagine Max looking so silly.

Ron joins us in the family room, "What's so funny you two?" His smile fills a room, just like Max's. There's no family resemblance, but the man stands and sounds so much like my future husband.

"I was just saying that I always wanted a kid sister." Jake sticks his tongue out once more.

"We're all happy to have you in the family, Lucy." Ron raises his coffee cup to me. Ron's definitely warmed up to me more on this trip. The first visit, he really intimidated me. Then learning about Max's past, I was even more scared of him. But both Ron and Alex have turned out to be very welcoming and nice to me. "We're looking forward to meeting your parents this week. I understand you have a brother that lives around here, too?"

"Yes. He and his wife with my two nieces live in Downers Grove."

"Good. Family's important to have around. Especially at times like these. Max said it'll be a small wedding, just your closest family and friends. But we look forward to meeting everyone."

Max had sent me up to bed last night again at 11:00. He must have stayed up talking more about me and the wedding. I blush thinking about what he might have said. *It seems like they know more about the wedding than I do.*

My phone buzzes next to me. I see it's a call from Laura. I didn't read this morning's texts yet, but I'd rather tell Laura first anyway. She's likely to be more excited for me at least...*hopefully.*

"Excuse me." I pick it up and head back upstairs, answering. "Hey, Laura."

"Wow! You finally picked up. Tracy, you can call off the dogs..." *Great, they're together. Well, two birds...*

"You guys are up early."

"Yeah. Big staff meeting. We're launching that new referral program, so it's all hands on deck, for the marketing department anyway. How are you?"

"I'm great actually."

"Oh? So...what happened Saturday?" I can tell that she's put me on speaker for Tracy to hear too.

I don't have anything prepared. I know what Max expects. He's been very clear about this. He expects me to tell the truth. *But I can't possibly tell them all that.* My face is beet red again. "Max was upset with me, but everything's fine now."

"Max was upset?! What about you?" Tracy is almost yelling into the phone.

"Where are you guys?" I really don't want my business broadcast in the office.

"We just got coffee around the corner. No one can hear us, Lucy...just tell us what happened." Laura is her usual nurturing self. I can tell that she's more worried than mad at me for ignoring all their attempts to reach me this weekend.

"There really isn't much to tell..." *a major white lie*, "I was wrong for letting Rich and that other guy think they could act like that with me and..."

"Lucy, do you hear yourself, for fuck's sake, quit with…" Laura obviously stops Tracy from interrupting.

"But Max and I are fine now," a blatant attempt to wash over everything. *But full speed ahead.* I take a deep breath, "Actually...better than fine. Max proposed yesterday!" There's absolutely nothing but street noise from their end. "So...I'm sorry that I didn't get back to you guys sooner...we've obviously been a little busy. My parents are really excited and his dad..."

"You said *yes*?!" Tracy's voice is almost as high as mine. I imagine her flaming red hair is paled by her face too.

"Of course."

"Oh my God. *You* talk to her...I can't even believe...I *can't* believe you!" Tracy is walking away from and back to the phone yelling into it.

"Stop yelling, people are looking at us!" Laura takes me off speaker. "Lucy...Um...so you are getting married?" She obviously doesn't know what to say, caught between Tracy's ranting in the background and my silence.

"Yes." I take a deep breath again. "Next month."

"Um...oh...that's crazy quick..." She's still trying to think of what to say, speaking slowly. In a whisper, "Are you...are you pregnant?"

I can hear another "Oh my God" from Tracy in the background. I nervously laugh, "No, no. We just don't want to wait."

"Wow." I wait for her to say something else, but she must have passed the phone to Tracy instead.

"Are you coming in today?"

"No. We're still in Wisconsin till this afternoon."

"Then we'll come over after work. We really need to talk." Tracy is all business and pissed off now.

"I...I'll have to see...we have a lot of plans to make, so I think I'm staying at Max's tonight..." I don't want to say that I have to ask Max's permission first to stay at my own place or to arrange seeing my friends. I feel a huge knot in my stomach and sit down on the bed.

"Fine. We'll see you there then." Tracy hangs up before I can say anything more. I just stare at my phone, unsure of what to do.

"Are you okay?" Jake is standing in the doorway. I jump again. He laughs, his hands up, "I swear I wasn't trying to sneak up on you. I thought you heard me come up the stairs."

"I don't know what to do..." I'm still staring at my phone in abject despair and uncertainty.

"About what?" Jake doesn't come into the room, but his large shoulders block the doorframe as he leans against it.

"My friends aren't too happy for me..." I don't want to get into the whole mess with Jake, but I don't want to be alone with my fear either. I'm afraid of what will happen when Max finds out that they're planning on coming over tonight and I didn't get his permission first. And I'm afraid of what they'll say later to me if they do come over. *What a mess!*

"Screw 'em then." He says this with a grin, but I can see that he's serious.

I laugh, it was exactly what I needed to hear. "Yeah...screw 'em!" And for a second, I mean it. But Tracy and Laura have been my best friends for two years. I'm closer with them than anyone. *Anyone except Max.*

"I'm heading back to the city. Will you tell Max that I'll call him this week to talk more?"

"Sure," he turns away, "and Jake? ...Thanks. You make a good big brother."

"Anytime, li'l sis."

My head feels clearer. *I have only one choice.* I can't please everyone. But I know that I need to please Max first. I send a text to Tracy and Laura together. "Tonight won't work. I really need to make some plans and I hope as my friends that you'll respect that. I will be in the office tomorrow, early. I love you both. xoxo"

Max will be proud of me. I head back downstairs to help with breakfast. *The morning light is so pretty on my ring. I am going to go blind staring at it.*

4 Him

"So your brother is going to pick your mom and dad up at the airport Thursday and they're going to stay with him over the weekend."

"Thank you." Lucy puts her arms out and I sit on the sofa pulling her onto my lap. I've been in the den on the computer coordinating with her dad. "You and your mom have an appointment to look at dresses on Friday and I'm going to take your dad out for a man-to-man talk." I say this extra machismo-y; she laughs.

"Please don't call it that to my dad. He'll make fun of you."

"What? Your dad already loves me."

"What's not to love?" She kisses my cheek. "I know for sure that my mom loves you."

"She just loves how much I love her daughter, baby." I kiss her a little longer.

"I can't believe you found a place that would guarantee a dress in less than four weeks. You do work fast, Mr. Traeger."

"I'm just determined to not let anything get in my way. You *will* be Mrs. Traeger next month." I kiss her forehead and pick up the checklist Lucy was working on. "So...what's next on your wedding to-do?"

"Only a guest list, invitations, find a place, get someone who can marry us, your tux, catering, flowers...Um...just a bazillion things!"

"Well...you are in luck, then. You happen to know a guy who's connected in the restaurant biz..."

"So where then?"

"I like the idea of my parent's place, but I think the weather could be tricky. October can be beautiful up there, but it's snowed before too. So I'm thinking it'll be somewhere in the city. I have a few ideas. I'll check around tomorrow." I kiss her nose and get up to grab the wine bottle from the dining table, pouring more into my glass. Lucy gives me a little pout for not pouring more for her.

"Lucy...take that pout off your beautiful mouth." She blushes and quickly changes to a small smile. "So...did you get a chance to talk to your friends today?"

"Yes...a little."

"You ignored your phone all weekend."

"I didn't want anything to disturb our time together..."

"I like that sentiment, baby, but we both know that isn't why you avoided your friends..." I'm a little stern with her.

"No. I didn't want to deal with them. I just wanted to be happy for a while. Is that so bad?" She's frowning again but quickly wipes it away.

"But you told them we're engaged, getting married in a month?"

"Yes."

"Good." I stand up and stretch. "Get ready for bed." I hold my hand out and she takes it while I pull her easily to her feet.

She looks at her watch. I know it's 11:00. "Are you coming too?"

"I'll be in soon. I'm going to track down a florist. Can't remember the guy's name, but he did a nice job at a wedding last year for a buddy of mine. I know he gave his info to the LPE Group to keep on file."

"Oh. Okay." She starts to walk towards the bedroom, but turns in the hallway. "Max?"

"Yeah?"

"Are you giving me a set bedtime?" Her look is perfect, only a little questioning.

I grin. "Yes."

"Oh. ...Okay."

I walk over to her and kiss her head, "I'll wake you when I come to bed..." and I turn into the den and close the door.

5 Her

I was going to save my "congratulations" cupcake from Jeff until after lunch, but I keep picking at it with my coffee. He was so sweet when he opened the car door for me and handed me the pink box, saying, "Ya gotta have cake to celebrate." And it's my favorite too, red velvet. He must have asked Max.

I was surprised at first that Jeff knew already. But Max has texted and called everyone. He's giving a heads-up that the wedding is right around the corner. So far, I've only told my family, Tracy, and Laura. I'm sure my mom has let the rest of the family know, so I'm covered there. And I have a few college friends and co-workers that I want to invite. Max said I have to give him my list tonight. He's having his assistant make out our invitations.

Since I'm in the office so early and no one else is around, I start on the list. I have to look up a few addresses, but I'm up to 25 pretty quickly. *Wow. I didn't even think I knew 25 people that well.*

"Aren't you a busy bee. Making up for slacking off yesterday, Lucy-Goose?" Kevin, my fellow recruiter, sets his bag down on his very neat desk. We've been officemates and co-conspirators against our boss for over a year; I add his name to the list.

"What's your address, Kev?"

"Why? My birthday was last month. Am I being served again? I told that cop that I didn't know that boy was underage...he *was* dancing in a cage at Chain Gang after all." Kevin loves to tease me with his raunchy stories, all made up. He's been in a committed relationship since before I knew him. But he decided that I was too "corn-fed" as he called it and needed some shocking. "Stop! What....is....thaaat?!" He points to my left hand.

"Oh, this is just my shiny new ring. You like it?" I twist and turn my hand in the air for him to see.

"Oh my God, girl. That ain't a ring, that's a strobe light!" Kevin comes bouncing over and grabs my hand. "At least four carats," he pretends to put on glasses, "Excellent cut and clarity, flawless color." He tries to take it off my hand and I smack his fingers. "Mr. Knight-in-Shining I presume?"

"Of course." I continue flicking my hand around in front of his face, making the diamond sparkle more in the ugly fluorescent lighting.

"And you want to invite moi to your wedding?" Kevin acts like he's tearing up and pulling a hanky from his shirt pocket.

"Of course. But since I know how busy you are with all the chain gang underage club thing...the wedding is next month."

Kevin looks me up and down in my chair. "Girl, you ain't showin' a bit!"

I hit his stomach. "I'm not pregnant."

"So what's the hurry? The engagement is the best part...ya get parties and presents and ya can still call the whole thing off if he pisses you off."

"We don't want to wait." I say this a little more defensively than I intended, but Kevin doesn't seem to notice.

"Well...count me in. I ain't missing the shindig that goes with *that* ring." He sits at his desk for a little while before saying, "Congrats, Lucy. I see how happy you are with Max and I'm happy for you."

I take another bite of my cupcake. *Now if I could just get my best friends to be as happy for me...*

It's noon before Tracy and Laura show up in my doorway. I've had to sit through two meetings and four interviews worrying about what they'll say, so by the time they peek their heads into my office, I'm a wreck. Tracy only sent back a curt text last night, "See you tomorrow."

"You ready for lunch?" Tracy sounds almost nice. I'm shocked.

"Yes...yeah...let's go." I grab my purse and follow them to the elevator.

On the street, Laura finally smiles at me. "So let's see the ring." I put out my left hand. "Oh my...It's so pretty."

"It's like a frickin billboard. Lucy's taken!" Tracy yells this on the sidewalk; Laura pushes her shoulder to get her to stop repeating it.

We're only getting to-go, since they both have busy meeting schedules, so I know this will be thankfully brief.

"So are you coming to Romona's tonight?" Tracy isn't saying much, but she's speaking volumes with her hostility.

"Yes." I already got Max's approval to go with them to our usual Wednesday night dinner. He told me to be back at his place by 9:30 and Jeff would be waiting outside with the car, but I can go at least.

"Good."

I know we'll talk more after work. For now, I got a congratulations out of Laura and one acknowledgement that the ring is nice out of Tracy. *It's a start.*

"Lucy, you got a sec?" Cruela pokes her head in and out of my office quickly. I jump up and follow her out into the hall, but stop suddenly when I see Rich waiting by an interview room door.

Cruela stands next to him, "Lucy, I know that you're busy today. But Rich requested that you sit in on a first interview for one of his new hires," she looks at her watch, "and you have a half hour free right now...so I agreed. Rich, let Lucy know if you need a formal feedback report or just a few notes, okay?"

Rich nods and Cruela takes off down the hall to terrorize someone else.

"So..." Rich blocks the door.

"I got your message the other night," I cut him off. "I did leave the party with Max. He's my fiancé." I put my left hand up to show the ring and Rich looks at his feet instead. "Well, we got engaged over the weekend..."

"Oh...well...that's great. Congratulations." He finally looks back up at me. "I just wanted to make sure you were okay...your *fiancé* seemed pretty angry about something."

I ignore this and point at the door. "I should get in there. I don't have a lot of time..."

"Oh...yeah. Bill could use your help. He tends to let the candidate get him sidetracked, so any pointers you can provide him, I'd appreciate it." Rich reaches with just one finger to touch my arm, but I move quickly to avoid this. "Thanks for doing this, Luce...maybe I could take you out for a celebratory drink sometime..."

"I don't think that'd be a good idea...but thanks." I just wait for him to finally move and knock on the door once before going in.

I try to concentrate on Bill's interview, but I'm distracted. Rich has always been friendly and he's joked about getting me on his team, but today he seemed more like a guy who missed out on a chance to date me. Max was right to be a little jealous of him I guess. I'm surprised that I didn't see Rich's interest before this. I *usually have such great instincts about people*.

"Oh my girls...all alone tonight, no guys?" Rosa is hovering over us as usual.

"No. We've had enough with guys lately..." Tracy shoots me a look.

"So, the usual then?"

We yell, "Yes," in unison. Rosa stops before going to give our order to her cooks though. "Is that...are you engaged, Lucy?"

I smile and put out my hand. It's about the thousandth time I've done this today. "Yes. Max and I are getting married next month." I've gotten used to saying the whole thing too.

"It's really nice. Congratulations, sweetie! Max is a really nice guy."

When she walks away, "If he's so nice, then why were you so scared of him Saturday?" Tracy is eyeing me over her glass of Chianti.

"I wasn't scared *of* him," hopefully she'll believe this technicality, "I was scared of *disappointing* him. I shouldn't have let another man touch me..."

"Why the hell not?! Who cares?" Tracy remains leaning back in her chair, but she's getting louder. Laura thankfully just stays quiet, looking between our tennis match.

"Because." I don't want to get into everything with them, so I opt for an easy answer, "*Because* Max is a jealous person and I know this. And I love him. I shouldn't have pushed him on this."

"Jealous? Try *insane*, Luce." She takes another big drink. I'd like to get drunk as usual on our Wednesday nights too, but I promised Max that I wouldn't. "Max grabbed your arms and looked like he was going to rip them off for God's sake."

Laura finally speaks up, but quietly, haltingly. "Lucy...we're just concerned that Max...well...he's...he's very controlling. And he seems to have a temper..."

"Well, I'm fine. All in one piece." I shake my arms at them. "See...nothing to worry about."

We all sit back in our seats, avoiding looking at each other for a minute. Rosa comes over with our breadsticks. "Hey...what's with the long faces? My girls are usually laughing so loud I have to remind you that there are other paying customers here."

We all smile up at her and I say a small, "Thanks," before she walks away shaking her head. "Look." and Tracy and Laura surprisingly both do, "I'm marrying Max. I love him and this *is* happening. So I need you two to get on board and be happy for me...*Please*?" I start to cry. I told myself that I wouldn't, but I'm a wimp.

Laura moves her chair closer to mine and puts her arm around my shoulder. Tracy grabs my hand from across the table, squeezing hard. "We've always got your back, Luce."

"Geez...I hope this isn't what you're planning for the bachelorette party." Rosa sets our spaghetti and meatballs down in the center of the table.

We laugh and I wipe my cheeks with my napkin while she serves our plates. The rest of the dinner is lighter. I tell them about how Max proposed and how our families reacted. Tracy doesn't make any more snide comments, just tries to be happy for me. She says she would never think of marrying anyone before she's thirty..."the Mark Twain-approved age for knowing thy true self" as she puts it. Laura said she was thinking of breaking it off with Tad and we talked about that for the next hour. It felt really good to be just normal and just us for a night.

"Max already took care of the check...you really are one lucky girl, Lucy...he's a keeper." Rosa walks away after leaving our tiramisu for us. I look at my watch guiltily at the reminder of Max. *Still plenty of time.* The diamonds from the watch sparkle up to match my ring. Two big reminders that I'm "Always" Max's just like the engravings on both.

6 Him

Smoke rings above our leather club chairs, filtering the low light more, tendrilling around the bookcases of wine behind us.

"I gotta say, I'm enjoying myself," Paul Sr. puffs a small circle into the air, "When you kids said you wanna get married next month, I thought you were crazy. Your mom just about threw a fit of crazy." He gestures with his cigar towards Paul Jr. who only nods, trying to make a ring himself. "But seeing how much you've already got done...well, I'm just glad that we can sit back like this and not be running all around town trying to figure out the craziness."

"I'm glad you can be here too, Sir. It was important to Lucy." I take another sip of my scotch, congratulating myself on thinking of this place. Nothing like a dark cigar bar, long stogies and tall drinks to bring future in-laws around. I'm glad Paul Jr. took the day off too. It'll be good that he's here for this talk as well.

"What's with this Sir...call me Paul...Hell, call me Pop," he's already a little tipsy I think, "You'll be a part of the family in a few weeks." PJ only nods again. He's definitely tipsy.

When our server comes in, I signal her for more water and to turn the fans on higher. We have the private tasting room, so the air will clear up quickly. That should help. I don't want to be responsible if they show up drunk later to dinner.

And I want to clear the air in other ways too.

7 Her

The buzzer sounds and I push on the door. There's a tiny elevator and stairs. We let Cathy take the elevator with the stroller and girls. Mom and I walk up and get to the second floor before her.

"I toldja they'd beat us!" My niece, Priscilla, is six and precocious. She runs into my arms and we laugh as I tickle her sides.

"Annie Oocy!" Her sister, Cassie, only two, has her arms up in the stroller for me to do the same to her. I bend down and tickle her a little, her giggles echo in the enclosed hallway.

The door opens and a very short, white-haired woman with very large dark glasses holds it open for us, "Miss Shannon?"

I'm not used to being addressed so formally, I blush a little at our loudness earlier. "Yes."

The light in the room is shocking after the darkened stairwell. There's white everywhere and crystal everywhere and a tall woman with equally white hair and large dark glasses coming forward to greet us. She's carrying a tray of drinks and hands one to each of us, champagne for Mom and me, orange juice for Cathy and the girls.

I smile. *Max thinks of everything*. He arranged this appointment and must have informed them who was coming with me and that Cathy is pregnant. *She's not showing yet, but she does glow*. I cheer with her first.

"I already have some specifications from Mr. Traeger and I've pulled a few choices for us to get started. Please, come with me. Ladies, have a seat on the sofa there and we will be right back." She very efficiently ushers me towards a room to the side. Mom and Cathy grin at us.

I'm too distracted with what specifications she means. Max doesn't want to see the dress, but he certainly cares a great deal about how I dress normally. I'm not surprised that he'd want a say in my wedding dress too.

There are three choices waiting for me. They are all bright white, all sparkling, all modest with big skirts.

"We will try this one first." She reaches for the nearest.

"Could...could I try one...that maybe isn't as...I don't know...big looking." I want to say isn't as covered-up looking. They all have long sleeves, high necks and backs.

"Mr. Traeger was very specific in what he wanted..." She gives me a knowing look. As if to say, he's paying her to make sure I get the dress that he'd approve.

Well, I don't need her to tell me what Max would like.
I've been following his rules of a how a good girl should dress
long enough to know. "Of course. But I know what Max likes
and I'd like to see a few other choices before starting...please."
She nods only once, putting the dress back on the wall. I try to
describe what I'm looking for and her face goes inward with a
frown with each word. It's definitely not the same as what's in
this room already. It's not up to Max's specifications.

Finally, she stops frowning and says she may have
something that we'd both like. She turns on a heel and leaves
before I can say anything more.

"What do you think?"

Mom has tears in her eyes and her hand to her mouth.
Cathy is smiling and the girls are clapping.

"Oh, Lucy...you look so beautiful!" Mom finally finds
her voice.

I look in the mirrors again. The dress is a perfect blend
between what I wanted and what Max specified. *At least I
hope it is.*

It's all white, all thick lace, no sparkle, with a soft
trumpet shape and a little train. The sleeves are tight lace
ending just above my elbows, the neckline is high, but follows
just below my collar bone, ending wide at the tips of my
shoulders. I turn a little. The back has a dramatic drop. *That's
definitely not to Max's specs, but I think he'll be okay with it.* I
chew my lower lip.

"What's the matter?" Cathy has stood up and is walking around the dress looking at the details.

"Do you think it's too sexy, open in back like this?"

"My God, girl, you're covered head to toe almost! Gotta show some skin, you're young."

"Mom...what do you think of the dress?"

"Your dad is going to cry when he sees you. It's perfect, sweetheart." She's standing next to Cathy now. My nieces give me thumbs up, but I'm still not sure.

I wish Alex was here...she'd know if Max would approve or not.

"Try on something else if you're not sure, but this almost fits you even." Cathy is sitting back down with Priscilla on her lap.

"It was a dress we ordered for a private runway show last year. My granddaughter is almost your size and she was supposed to model it, but she was sick last minute. So, it's never even been tried on before. It needs a few alterations, but yes...it does suit you." The efficient pronouncement makes up my mind.

"I'll take it."

"Sweetheart, you didn't get the price..." Mom whispers this, but I don't know why since we're the only ones in the shop and Ms. Efficient already walked away to get her seamstress. And she knows Max is paying for everything; he had that talk last night with Dad at PJ's house.

"Max told me not to worry about that, just to get the dress I like best," I smile at myself in the mirror. It's not exactly what I pictured, but I do feel very grown-up, pretty, and, turning a little again, sexy too.

"Well...you look great." Cathy is holding Priscilla's thumbs up.

I laugh, "And at least in a dress this form-fitting everyone won't be asking if I'm pregnant at the wedding."

"Lucy…" Mom acts shocked by this, although she asked me too in private last night.

"Now. The little girls' dresses. Pink or white?" Ms. Efficient has returned with three helpers, all white-haired, all big glasses. *It's a wedding-shop-cult.* I have to stop myself from laughing, but Cathy just cracks up on the sofa, covering her face in her daughter's hair.

"Pink!" Priscilla answers for us.

"Pink it is." I nod seriously at my niece. Cathy gets up and goes back with the girls, still giggling.

The seamstress starts tucking and pulling, twisting me this way and that, arms up, arms down. I feel like I'm already doing a chicken dance.

"Mom, Max said he'd be happy to get you a dress from here too, if you'd like." She's watching the seamstress very carefully and putting her two cents in when she thinks something is too tight. The woman is completely ignoring her.

"Oh, no. I don't need anything this fancy... Do I?" She's looking around the room uncomfortably.

"Well, his parents are pretty formal people. Maybe you should try on some things... We're here..."

And another white-haired helper appears out of nowhere. I can't help but laugh this time. *Where are they coming from?* The seamstress clucks her disapproval from my feet. I stop moving before I get pinned to the floor.

8 Him

"Sir...Paul," I smile when he nods, "I'm glad we have this time to talk, just man to man." He sits up a little more in his chair. PJ sits back in his. "I love your daughter very much." He nods again with a smile. "And I will take very good care of her."

"You better!" He points with his cigar and a fake stern look.

"And I want you to know we will have a *very* traditional marriage." I watch his face change from a grin to a confused smile. I keep mine neutral, waiting for him to say something. PJ's face is equal parts amused and confused, watching us both.

"Um...what do you mean by traditional, Max?" Paul asks slowly. He's a little tipsy, but I can tell he's trying to match my earnest tone.

"I was raised in a very traditional home... My father was the head of the house, the rest of us obeyed his rules without question. My home will be the same." I again wait for the change in his expression. I think Lucy must get this from her dad. His smile moves quickly from confused, to a grin, back to confused, settling on a hard half smile.

"And Lucy knows this...that this is what you want?"

"Yes, Sir."

PJ laughs, but Paul only shakes his head, "My daughter can be pretty headstrong. I find it hard to believe that she wants a very traditional anything..."

"You can ask her yourself, Sir. I wanted to clear the air, though...before the wedding. I think it's important that you know the kind of man that's marrying your daughter."

"I do too. I appreciate you talking to me like this, Max. But I...well, I just don't know what to say to you..." He takes a drink and puts his cigar in the ashtray, "I think you're setting yourself up for disappointment, frankly. And I want to see my daughter happy."

"I will make Lucy very happy, Paul." I raise my glass to this and both men clink theirs to mine.

9 Her

"Are we doing parties?"

"Parties? You mean like a bachelor, bachelorette kinda thing?"

"Yes. Cathy asked me yesterday if we were doing all the traditional stuff...registering for gifts, having a shower and parties."

"And how did you answer?" He's eyeing me sideways, his hand still loosely on my knee. We're on our way to his parent's house in Evanston.

"I said that I wasn't sure we'd have time for all that..." I add quietly, "and that I needed to check with you."

"Good girl." He squeezes my knee and I giggle a little. "Dan asked me the same thing. I think he's planning something for next weekend." He looks over at me again, but quickly puts his eyes back on the road. "You may have a party next Saturday."

"Thank you!" I'm nervous about tonight, but the thought of everything coming together so quickly and easily has me feeling a little more relaxed.

Tonight is the meeting of the families. *Cue big scary theme music in my head*. Max said he had a nice time yesterday with my dad and brother, but this is a little different. I haven't even been to this house yet.

It's what I was expecting. Big, all brick, craftsman style with a large porch. I don't see PJ's car yet, so we're the first to arrive.

Ron opens the door for us and takes the wine from Max, hugging me. "Alex is in the kitchen..." I take this for what it is...directions. I smile at Max and he nods towards a large dining table and door. I guess I'm getting used to being ordered around by the Traeger men and getting permission to leave the room. *But it still feels damn weird*! I smile at my naughtiness...*I can still get away with cursing in my own head at least*. I mentally stick my tongue out at Ron. *Max may want me to be obedient even inside my own head, but I can still entertain myself.*

"Oh, honey, thank goodness. I was hoping you'd get here before your mom. I'm running behind...can you help with the stove?" Alex gives me a handless hug, holding a large fork and knife away from me. "Just stir everything."

"Sure." I step out of her way as she puts the large roast back in the oven. I help with stirring and whipping. "This all smells and looks wonderful, Alex. Thanks for doing this."

"Of course. We have to give your parents and family a proper welcome from ours."

"Well my dad is going to love you...this is his favorite."

"I usually make this on Sundays, but Ron let me make it today instead."

The casualness of her statement still surprises me. I don't know if I'll ever get used to saying things like "let me" in front of other people.

Max pokes his head in, "Your family's here, baby." Alex wipes her hands on her apron and takes it off, smiling at me and following Max out.

Ron is already shaking hands with PJ and Cathy, they left the kids with her sister though. Mom and Dad are moving into the living room. Mom's eyes are big taking in how nice the place is. She walks over to me with an impressed smile.

Everyone says hello to Alex too. I hang back, just comparing our parents. Mom is a little shorter than Alex, a little older. Mom is in nice pants; Alex is in a dress of course. Dad is about the same height as Ron, both men have salt and pepper hair. But Dad's not as fit as Ron. Everyone seems happy congratulating each other.

PJ puts his arm over my shoulder. "The nightmare begins, sis." I slap his stomach. "Now you will know the joy of splitting all your time between two sets of parents." He laughs.

"Please excuse me, I have to finish dinner." No one else noticed the subtle nod Ron gave her before she says this, though.

Max only looks at me and says quietly, "Lucy..." nodding towards his mom.

"I'll help." I quickly turn around and follow her, not wanting anyone to see me blushing.

"Everyone seemed to get along great tonight," I'm sleepy and put my head back against the headrest with my eyes closed.

"I thought so too." Max strokes my cheek with the back of his fingers. "You were very good tonight."

"*You* were very bossy tonight." I open my eyes a little to peek at him.

He only grins more. "Yes. I had a talk with your dad yesterday. I wanted him to see for himself that you're happy with how things are between us."

"What did you say to him...?" I swallow. *I wish I'd known about this earlier.*

"Nothing specific. I just wanted him to understand that our home will be different from the one you were raised in." He looks over at me, a little sternness back in his eyes. "Your mom contradicts your dad a lot and he lets her get away with it."

"Well...she doesn't mean anything by it. I mean she's only voicing her own opinions after all..."

"It's not my place to say anything about *their* marriage. I only say it as a point that you were raised thinking that a wife can argue with her husband; I wanted your dad to know that won't be *our* marriage." I don't say anything, so he continues, "My dad asked me again tonight if I'm sure that you're ready to be my wife."

"He asked you that? And he's asked before?"

"Yes. He asked me the night before I proposed."

"And what did you say?"

"I told him then that I knew you were the one for me. That I know that I've rushed us, but I know in my heart that we'll make each other happy. And even after seeing more how your family is together tonight, I know that you're the one."

"You make my family sound bad..."

"No." He squeezes my hand. "But tonight I saw more how your mom and dad are together, how your brother is with his wife. I know what I'm demanding of you is different from what you've always known." He pulls into his garage, so he stops talking while he parks.

In the elevator, he picks up where he left off, though, pulling me into a hug.

"Lucy, I'd like to say that I'll go slow with you, that I'll ease you into being my wife. But we both know that isn't my style." He gives me a crooked grin and I touch his cheek.

"No. Certainly hasn't been so far..."

"And you've done very well with all my rules and discipline. But I'm not going to go easy on you just because you weren't raised to be a proper, obedient girl." He kisses my forehead, so my shocked look is covered.

"My parents raised me to be a good girl, Max." *I don't like that he's disparaging how I was raised.*

With his head bent down to mine still, his voice takes on the edge that makes my pussy pulse, "And that right there is what I'm talking about, little girl. You still think you can get away with arguing with me. Don't you?"

"I'm...I'm not arguing...I just...I don't like that you're saying something bad about how I was raised."

He drops his arms and the doors open. *I have a bad feeling about how this night is ending...*

10 Him

"Undress and face the wall." I don't stop to look at her, just head down the hall into the kitchen. I pour myself a scotch and take a deep drink.

My temper flares so quickly with her! I've never known this feeling with previous girlfriends. *True, I've never cared this much for a girl. She will be my wife and I won't have us starting off the wrong way*. I take a few deep breaths and another sip before walking back into the hall.

She stands just as I've taught her, close to the wall, nude, hands clasped behind her back, stomach tight, head up. *She's so beautiful.* Her long blonde curls cover her shoulders and back. Her tits rise shakily from her attempt to calm her own breathing.

I don't say anything just walk slowly up to her, standing just a little to her left, but close enough that her fingertips brush against me. I grab her hair and yank her head back fast, keeping my fingers tightly wound in curl. She stares into my eyes.

Her bright blue eyes, so telling. *Fear*. I pull her hair more and she squeaks. I kiss her hard and she responds as always. *Hungry*.

"Follow." I walk slowly into the bedroom and stand next to the bed. She stands a little away from me, but quickly takes two steps closer when I look at her.

"You can't seem to hold your tongue and behave, little girl."

"I'm sorry, Sir. Please...can we...can we talk. *Please, Max*."

"No." I watch as her look goes from shock to despair. I know she's fighting her urge to say something more, so I give her time. "*We* aren't talking about anything, Lucy. You are *listening*. *I* am talking. Do you understand?"

"...Yes, Sir." Her voice is soft and pouty.

"I won't have you thinking that you can talk back to me like your mom does to your dad. I won't have you thinking that you can get away with contradicting me like your brother's wife does to him." My anger is flaring back up, my voice getting deeper and quieter. "You weren't raised properly, Lucy." I don't have to wait long for the defiance to surface in her expression again. I grab her face, fingers gripping her cheeks and I like that her eyes are quickly changed to shock. Her hands stay behind her back though.

"You weren't raised to be obedient. You don't know your place, little girl." I let go of her face. "Get the belt." She goes slowly to the closet and brings the belt back to lay on the bed in front of me.

"Bend over the bed." She hesitates. I've only spanked her standing up or over my knees so far, so she's uncertain what to do. But she lowers her hands and puts them on the bed, shoulder length apart. "Keep your legs together and your back arched." I rub my hand down her back and over her ass. She shivers.

"You were going to have a light maintenance spanking tonight, Lucy. But you blew that, little girl." She shivers again and starts to say something. "No. I don't want to hear another word out of your mouth except 'yes, sir' or 'no, sir'. Do you understand me, Lucy?"

"Yes, Sir."

"You will not speak for the rest of tonight or all day tomorrow. Your mouth got you into this trouble, maybe not using it will help you to think before you speak. And if you say anything besides 'yes or no, sir' we will be right back here for a harsher spanking. Do you understand me?"

"...Yes...yes, Sir." She knows she's angered me. Her fear is electric.

"I'm going to hit you ten times with the belt." Her ass clenches at this news. She remembers the last time I was angry and spanked her at the party. I rub her back and ass again and say slowly, "If I hear anything from you more than a small cry, I'll start over."

Thinking about the maintenance spanking, remembering how angry I was last week, I get even more control over my temper. I'm angry, but I am in control of it. *And I want to enjoy this spanking.*

I double the belt and take a deep breath. She's so beautiful, waiting. My cock is already painfully aroused. I place the first whack high on her ass. It's not too hard, but she's sensitive here. She bounces on her toes and muffles her cry to a hiss between her teeth. The pink print is so nice, I imagine kneeling and kissing it.

The next whack is dead center on her right cheek. It's a little harder; she can take it here. She keeps her cry behind closed lips. The mark is a little angrier in color.

I give her another dead center hit, left cheek. Same beautiful mark appears.

My favorite, lowest part of her cheeks, the belt hits both sides at once, a good hard smack. She dances and hardly keeps her cry contained.

I raise the belt and know her eyes are closed; she doesn't tense, just waits. I land two stripes across the side of each cheek quickly, more stinging than hard, bringing the belt down across my body.

She bounces again, her cry more an open mouth moan now. I listen to her breathing. Her arms are shaking. Her ass is now painted with beautiful, pink cherry stripes.

The last two I deliver quickly, one on top of the other, a little low. She almost blows it and has to gulp back her cry two times. Her back heaves with the effort to stay still and quiet against the pain.

"On the bed, on your hands and knees." She climbs onto the bed. "Keep your legs together." I push her forward onto her elbows. Her ass is a perfect prize offered to me.

I think about fucking her in her ass. But that's a punishment I'll keep for another time. *One where I'm not ready to explode just watching her back move with her heavy breathing.*

I pull her cheeks apart and shove myself into her pussy. She's wet, but I didn't open her, her tightness resists and I pull out and in quickly. She puts her face to the bed to hide her deeper moan.

I grab her shoulder and push in harder, my own moan loud. She's never been able to take all of me, not without a little pain. *I love filling her.*

I use her shoulder to keep her close and only pull out a little. She squeezes me and I almost lose it. *God, she's so hot.* I push into her hard. We moan together. I pull out a little; she squeezes, her back arching more, her panting louder between her teeth. I push in deeper. We do this three more times. But I can't wait longer. I let go of her shoulder and grab her hips. I fuck her fast and hard, yelling out when we come, head back.

I pull out and sit back on my heels. Her pink ass and wet cunt are almost eye level. She's still panting. I lightly kiss her left cheek, then her right before getting out of bed.

11 Her

Rolling over, I can tell Max is up already. I've gotten used to sleeping naked with him. His body heat keeps me toasty warm all night. Now the sheets feel too cold and I get up.

He left me a note in the kitchen. "Went for a run. We'll go out for breakfast. You'll get your phone back tomorrow. Love, M." I walk over to the hallway and look in my purse. He took my phone.

Because I can't talk today. I laugh out loud, a single harsh laugh. I feel strange. Oddly okay with it.

I shouldn't be okay with it, should I? Last night, I knew Max was upset with me and his declaration that I wasn't allowed to speak today seemed like a nightmare. *This morning...I dunno....I'm oddly okay with it.*

Why, though? I don't have any knots in my stomach...I don't even feel any anger that he took my phone or expects me to obey his command, "Thou shalt not speak!"

I grab a cup of coffee and head back into the bedroom to dress, still trying to figure out my strange okay-ness.

Inspecting myself in the bathroom mirrors, I see a few red marks from last night's punishment. And I'm not even phased by them. I've gotten used to seeing myself with Max's marks on me. I've gotten used to all of his rules and consequences if I break any of them.

I put the washcloth over my mouth like a gag. *I've gotten used to being this new me... Is that why I'm okay with this new punishment? It's just another mark, invisible tape over my mouth?*

I realize that I haven't spoken out loud to myself even though Max isn't here to hear me. *And that's why I'm okay with it...because it's me deciding to be?*

The other punishments, I've had to submit to them. But Max could easily have forced them on me too. He'd have no problem holding me down for a spanking. *But this...this is different.* He's not gagging me. He's trusting that I'll obey him. He's telling me what he wants, and it's entirely up to me to give it to him.

I know if I don't obey him, there are consequences. I absently rub my butt at this thought. *But even that, I'd be submitting to again.*

I've been thinking about what he said last night. I know Max doesn't think badly of me or my family. He said he really likes all of them. *But he's right that I wasn't raised like he was. My dad wasn't king of any castle, like Ron is.* I was able to get away with a lot as a kid. Mostly, I thought because I was raised more-or-less as an only child, since there's fifteen years between PJ and me. Or because my parents wanted to have a lot of kids and I was their last hope.

Now, I'm seeing that it might have been because my mom was so indulgent of me. And she never really let my dad step in to discipline. *Not that I was a bad kid...I hardly did anything in comparison to some of my friends.* But, still...there were only a few times that I was spanked or even grounded as a kid.

I laugh again, but to myself. *I've been grounded, spanked, slapped, and put in a closet by Max. And now I have invisible tape. And I'm okay with all of it.*

I want to please Max. I want to give him everything that he demands. I want to bend to his will. And if that means not speaking today, I can do that.

My past boyfriends have all been "normal" guys. They didn't demand too much of me. But I realized in the first month with Max that this side of me, this need to please, has always been there. I do it at work, with friends, with family. *I try to please everyone.*

I don't push back when my boss gives me impossible deadlines or adds more work to my plate. I took over the cross-training with the accounting department recruiters because I wanted to impress Cruela. And I wanted her to be pleased with me. *I don't think that woman is happy with anyone. But I tried...*

And I always give in to Tracy. *She's a force of nature.* She doesn't even realize how bossy and demanding she is. Laura and I both give in to her all the time, do what she wants to do.

It's just natural to me to be this people-pleaser. The closest thing to doing what I wanted instead of what someone else did is when I decided to stay in business instead of nursing like Mom wanted. She was disappointed, but I don't think she really believed it mattered. Just get a degree, get a husband, have babies was her plan for me.

And I guess that's exactly what I'm doing...still pleasing her. Hearing Max say that she isn't the kind of wife he'd want really upset me last night. I've modeled myself after her, tried to live up to what she wanted for me, *from* me.

I always thought Mom deferred to Dad, that she was a little old-fashioned herself. She didn't work outside the house, she hated any use of bad language, and liked to think of herself as the etiquette queen. But when push came to shove, she really was the one who made all decisions.

And I've never really wanted that in a relationship...to be the decision-maker. I smile at myself. I'm wearing a light yellow dress and sweater. *Dressed just the way Max would like.* Only with Max, have I had this kind of relationship...*free to just be happy in making him happy.* Despite all of his rules, this is all that really matters to him.

I have to let Max make all the decisions for us. I have to trust that he'll make choices that are good for both of us. *I have to bend to his will for both of us to be happy.*

I hear the front door close and I jump up to greet him. *Silently, of course.* I smile to myself, feeling that familiar pulse from my stomach to my pussy that obeying him gives me.

12 Him

"You were a very good girl today." Lucy is snuggled in a ball on my lap. She's been needing extra attention all day, keeping a connection between us.

I've missed hearing her voice. This punishment has been torture for me. She's giggled and laughed, but the sweetness of my Lucy has been locked away behind her closed lips all day. It's taken all of my will not to give in and let her speak again. *She needs to learn this lesson though.*

She managed not to speak all through breakfast. Well...I do the ordering anyway, but she only politely smiled at the waiter whenever he brought her anything.

We just got back from shopping for good running shoes for her. She wasn't happy about it, but she remained quiet.

"I signed you up to start jogging at the gym around the corner." She tries to hide her little frown by lowering her head more. "The track is good for beginners and you can pace yourself. I ordered a pedometer for you too. You'll keep track of your distance and time in a log that you'll show me every Saturday. When you're ready, we'll be able to run together. Would you like that?"

"Yes, Sir." She manages to put a lot of pout into those two words.

"I also signed us up for an Art Institute membership." Her smile is genuine this time. I know this is her favorite museum. "It'll be a fun thing for us to do together. Just like running will be."

"Yes, Sir." She sounds a little more convinced this time.

"We have three weeks until our wedding. The invitations are going out tomorrow, but I think everyone who's invited has already been informed. I have rooms reserved for our families just a block from the restaurant. And I've booked our honeymoon." She looks excitedly at me, questioning with her whole face to tell her the destination. "Nope...it's a surprise." She slaps my shoulder playfully.

"That leaves one last item of business before our wedding." She looks wary and questioning. "You need to give your two week notice tomorrow." I ignore her shocked look. "This will give you one full week before the wedding to pack up your apartment and work on any final arrangements. I've made all the plans, but you will need to make sure that they all happen how I've specified." Her look is still shocked. I know she wants to say something, her mouth keeps opening and closing, her eyes searching my face, her hands gripping the skirt of her dress.

"I'll be busy with clearing up my schedule for our honeymoon. I have a few cases to hand off at the firm and some loose ends with LPE business to handle. The next few weeks, I'm going to be working late and won't be able to provide the wedding details much of my attention."

I like watching her suffer with this. She wants so badly to say something, but she knows if she does what will happen.

"Of course, I'll make time to administer your maintenance spankings." A little reminder of consequences helps her to quiet again. "You have two week's worth coming. One for yesterday and one for last week still." I wait for her to acquiesce. When she only continues fidgeting with her hands and searching my face, I give her a sterner look and put a little of the impatience I feel into my voice. "Lucy..."

"Yes, Sir." *My good girl.*

13 Her

"I really have to quit today?...I mean...I could...please, Max, reconsider. I could work until...well...if we have a baby, then I could see. But we're not even married yet..." I've said all of this quietly in the most respectful tone I can think of, but I can still see that I've angered him.

I tossed in my sleep all night. Max said I was mumbling too, but he joked that he wouldn't hold that against me. *Gee, thanks*. I'm a wreck thinking about quitting. I don't make eye contact with him, just keep my eyes looking out the window at the passing storefronts.

"Lucy, I understand that you're trying. I know you want to be respectful and you're figuring out your limits. And I want to help you." His hand moves my chin gently back to look at him, but his voice is edgier. "Look at me when I'm talking to you." He drops his hand and I keep my eyes on him while he continues. "You may ask me to reconsider a decision, but giving me your reasons for wanting me to is tantamount with arguing. Try again."

I swallow. *I want Max to reconsider because I don't see the need to quit right now. Because I like my job and I'm good at it. But I can't say any of that.* I swallow again. We're almost to my building. "Max, please reconsider letting me quit later, not today...please."

"Much better." He gently strokes my cheek and I can smell his soap and lineny-male muskiness that makes me want to crawl on him and bite his neck. I'm distracted from my problem for the moment and I lean in to give him a kiss. I'm rewarded with a bigger smile.

He continues talking, with the smile still in place, "You *are* quitting today, Lucy." My horny glazed look fades from my eyes and I am left with disappointment. *He didn't even think about it!* "I've given this a lot of thought already. You knew that this day would come; I told you that I wasn't going to allow you to work forever." He did say this, but I didn't think it would be before we had kids. "And I won't have my wife working outside of my home. You will be busy enough just being my wife. And now *is* the time with the wedding right around the corner and last minute details to take care of."

The car stops and Jeff gets out to open my door for me. I start to look away, but stop turning my head when he continues, "I won't always explain my decisions like this to you." His smile goes crooked. "Because I said so is going to be enough explanation for you, little girl."

"...Yes, Sir."

"I will be working late tonight. Jeff will pick you up and take you to your place to get started on packing." He leans over and gives me a deep kiss. Despite the knot in my stomach, I yield to his tongue and feel a little lightheaded when I stand up.

I close the door. Cruela took the news better than I thought. *She was a complete sarcastic bitch about it, but better than I thought.* She made a snide comment about me becoming some society wife with servants. I'm glad I chose not to invite her to the wedding now.

The bad news is she wants my last two weeks to be spent training the accounting recruiters. And that means working closely with Rich again. She said that she might as well get some use out of me for as long as she can and Rich's new hires could still use some help.

I take a deep breath. *Now to tell Kevin. And Tracy and Laura.* The knot just keeps getting bigger in my stomach.

"Knock, knock." Rich stands in my doorway, a small smile on his face. "I just got out of a meeting with Catherine. She says you're going to be helping out my team again...at least for two weeks." He comes to lean on my desk right next to me.

I already told Kevin, just before his first interview. He was pretty upset, but then made a joke about not working either if he could find the right man. I wish he was here for this; I feel uncomfortable being alone with Rich. *Guilty*.

"Word travels fast around here." I move my chair a little away from him.

"So...how bout we go to lunch today to put together a game plan...?" He's still smiling at me, leaning in.

"Um...well...I have lunch plans...how bout we meet at 1:00? I have a few interviews still lined up this afternoon, but I think Catherine is reorganizing my schedule to free me up."

"All right, it's a date." He turns and walks away. *This is going to be a stressful two weeks.*

"Can't you just be happy for me?" We've been arguing all through lunch. Tracy keeps saying the same things over. She hardly lets me speak while harping on about how Max is too controlling, how I shouldn't give up my job, how I should be independent and think for myself...blah blah blah. It's her same tune about not liking Max at all.

I take a deep breath and try to make her understand this from my perspective. I interrupt her latest rendition, "Tracy. You're my best friend and I love you." She shuts up at least. "But I need you to understand that I don't take orders from you. I am living my life the way I want and I want you to be happy about it for me."

Laura just stares at me. Since being with Max, I've put my foot down more with Tracy. I've not let her dominate the conversations, not let her push us around to doing what she wants to do all the time. This restaurant is a perfect example. Tracy doesn't like this place, but Laura and I do. But we hadn't been here in over six months. The last time was when Tracy was out sick for the afternoon.

Tracy just blinks like she doesn't recognize me. She answers in a calmer and quieter voice, "But you *do* take orders from Max. Is that what you call living your life?"

"Yes." Both are blinking at me. I don't say anymore, just get up with my cup to refill it with more water. When I return to the table, I pick up my purse, saying, "I have to get back for a meeting with Rich..."

Laura starts to get up too, but Tracy remains sitting. "He likes you, you know?"

"Who? Rich?" *I don't want to hear this*. The guilty knot is returning and my stomach is way too full to deal with that.

"Yeah. He confessed to me that he likes you at the party." Tracy keeps watching me. "He said he went looking for you. That he was worried about you..."

I only shake my head and continue walking away. Tracy gets up and quickly comes after me though, "And only a few months ago, you would've been so happy to hear that news. I know you liked him too..."

I turn on her as soon as we're out the door. "And it doesn't matter anymore, Trace. I'm with Max. I'm getting *married* to Max. And I won't see Rich after two weeks from today." I don't wait for her to respond; I just walk away with Laura closely at my side. Tracy doesn't follow us.

"You really want to quit?" Laura isn't angry like Tracy. She genuinely wants to know that I'm okay.

"Yes." I stop for a second; we were both walking too fast. "I knew marrying Max would mean that I wasn't going to need to work." *A slight blurring of the truth.*

"But...you're okay with quitting *now*? I always assumed that if I had kids, I wouldn't want to work too. But until you are *large* with child..." she puts her hands out in front of her stomach, laughing. *She's so sweet, trying to make a joke to make me feel better.* I laugh lightly too.

"I'm sure I'll have plenty to keep me busy just getting used to being a wife before that happens." And I realize that this is what Max had said. *And I'm afraid to think of what he meant by it.*

I'm actually happy to be heading to my place, alone. Today has given me a headache. My neck felt like it was a twig waiting to snap. *Everyone asked about my quitting. I had to meet with Rich...I don't even want to think more about that. Tracy. Cruela.* All added to the strain on my twiggy neck.

I'm just glad to have this time to myself. I realize that it's been weeks since I've slept in my own bed. I think of Max's place as our home already. *Well, it is a lot bigger and nicer.*

I open the door and there's a light on inside. *Shoot, I must have left it on all this time.*

There's a note on my coffee table. "I've left boxes for you. Please pack only what you really need or want. The rest will be donated. No furniture, unless it's of sentimental value to you. Love, M."

I look beyond the small apartment and see boxes stacked between my bed and dining area. *Max does think of everything.* He's already paid off my landlord for the rest of my lease. *All I have to do is decide what pieces of my old life will go with me...*

And I'm actually surprised that this makes me so sad. *I didn't think about leaving this place.* I'll be leaving my things behind. I felt so proud of myself for finding this place on my own, for decorating it the way I wanted...*well, the way I could afford at least*. I liked having my stuff all around, messy or clean, it was up to me.

I know in Max's house, nothing will be up to me. *I've come to terms with that. I think so anyway.* But I still feel a sadness at giving up so much. At *having* to give up so much, in order to gain so much more. *And I know my life with Max will be more...more love, more fulfilling, more of what I want...* But still it sucks to look around here and realize that not much is going to go with me.

I lay on my bed and close my eyes.

I'm bolted up by a knock on my door. *Probably Jeff.* He said he wasn't going to wait, just to text him when I'm ready to leave, but he must've changed his mind. We both know I have a 9:30 curfew.

"Hey! What are you doing here?"

"Nice to see you too." Laura is pushing her way into my apartment. She has a pizza and wine with her. "Max called me this afternoon. Said you might like some company and help packing up your stuff."

He does think of everything. I start to cry.

Laura puts the box and wine down quickly and puts her arms around me. "Oh, sweetie...why are you crying? What happened?"

Moving out of her arms, I wipe my eyes and take a deep breath. "Oh, God, Laura. I don't even know why I'm crying!" I pick up the wine and she grabs the pizza, following me into the kitchen. "This is all happening so quickly...I think my head is just spinning."

"So...slow things down. You don't have to rush into getting married..."

"Yes. I do." She looks at my stomach again and I hit her lightly on the shoulder. "No. I mean..." I take a deep breath. *I need to talk to someone*. "Can I be totally honest with you...and you won't judge me for it?"

"Like you even have to ask!" But she can see that I'm not going to say anything unless she actually says it. "Yes...I won't judge you. You know that."

She takes two plates with pizza and I take two glasses and the wine into the dining area. The boxes are staring at us. *Jury boxes*.

"I wouldn't be able to say this to Tracy. But I...I need someone to talk to, Laura." She squeezes my arm and I continue. *What the heck, right?* "I don't have a choice about getting married in a few weeks. I didn't have a choice about quitting today."

"What do you mean? Why not?"

"Because you're right...about Max. He is very controlling. He told me to quit and I did." *There I said it*. I sit back and take a big drink, not looking at her. Above the rim of my glass though, I can see that she hasn't moved.

"But...but it's not like *you* didn't do it...I mean he didn't have a gun to your head, right?" She's trying to joke; I know she's unsure of what to say to me.

"Yes...I had to choose to do it...to *obey* him." I say this as a whisper.

She only swallows her wine with a gulp at this. She keeps looking at me, then at her plate. "And that's why you were crying...because you don't want to...to obey him?" she says this awkwardly.

"No...Well...I just felt all the stress of today, of the last few months really...I dunno." I shake my head, laughing at myself. "I cried because you're my best friend and you'd want to be here for me. Because Max is so sweet that he'd know that I need somewhere here for this part. Because I've been keeping all of this to myself and I just needed to get it out. I needed to be honest with you."

"Well...I'm glad that you are. I just...wow! What do I say?" Laura is smiling at me, a little mystified at my rambling. She's usually the rambler.

"You don't have to say anything..."

"But..." She sits up a little more, puts her wine glass down and looks at me squarely. "Do you really love Max? Do you really want to marry him?"

"Yes." I don't hesitate in my answer. *I know this is true.*

"Then...then you're *okay* with how controlling he is?"

"Yes." I'm shy about this answer only because I don't want her to judge me for it.

"Then...then that's all that matters I guess." She squeezes my arm again, but continues to look intently at me. "I had a guy I dated for a while. It was before I knew you. He was kinda like that. I think about him sometimes still..."

"What happened with him?" Laura hasn't really told me much about previous guys. I know she broke things off with Tad. She said he just wasn't right for her, even though he made her laugh a lot.

"It was college. He switched majors and schools. He tried to get me to go with him, but my folks couldn't afford out of state tuition. We stayed in touch for a while, but we just drifted apart..." She shrugs, "But stupidly I've compared other guys to him since then. If they aren't that into me like he was..." She shrugs again.

"I don't think that's stupid. You know what you want and you're not willing to settle, that's all." I pour more wine for us both.

"And *is* Max what you want?"

"Yes." This time I'm smiling. "I've never known anyone like him before. But he's what I've always wanted that's for sure."

"Good." She's smiling too. "And you said he has a brother...?" She's giggling. I push her shoulder and we both start laughing again.

14 Him

"So...are you going to make good on our deal or what?"
We're standing outside the bar, getting away from all the party
fun for a moment. Dan went crazy planning this thing.
Strippers of every shape and rainbow have been dancing
around for the last hour. I laughed at the first couple, but now
it's just overkill. "And when are you going to quit smoking?" I
wave away some smoke moving on the air towards me.

"I'm working on it. Both those things!" Mike blows more
smoke straight up into the air and laughs. "I swear you just
proposed so quick to make me look bad."

Dan joins us, taking a hit off of Mike's cigarette. Dan
thinks it's okay to smoke as long as he didn't buy it. We all
know that Becca wouldn't agree with him. "Yeah. He's getting
married, so you'll have to propose to Stephie finally. That
sounds like Max."

I give Dan a nod back towards the door and he questions with his brows for a second. He finally gets it and just turns to walk back into the bar.

"Mike. There's something that I've been wanting to talk to you about."

Mike smiles, "Let me guess...I'm not the best best-man right?"

I laugh. "I have to give that to Jake. You and Dan are both best-men though." I clap him on the shoulder. "No. I need to talk to you about the wedding. Well, about Lucy and me."

He doesn't say anything, just snubs out his cigarette on the ground and turns to face me more. "I had this talk with Dan already. That night Jake split with Julia. But I haven't really had a chance to talk to you..."

"Okay. You got my curiosity going..."

"It's about the type of relationship I have with Lucy. The type of *marriage* I'll have with her." I pause just to see if he's going to make some joke, but he seems to pick up that I need him to be serious for a moment. "I know you know that my dad was strict with Jake and me." He nods his head like this is an understatement. "Yeah. It was his way or no way growing up and we all toed the line. That included my mom." His expression doesn't change. "And I am the same way with Lucy."

His expression turns funny, like I just made a joke that he doesn't quite get yet. "Are you into some sort of bondage sm thing...cuz I can recommend a few clubs in the area if you are...?" He laughs, but I've known him long enough to see that he's serious too.

I can feel that my own look has gone a little comical in response. "Good to know. But no. That's not what I mean...well...?" I shrug and laugh again. "No. I mean that...well to be blunt about it; I'm in charge and Lucy toes the line. It's not a sex or playing around thing. It's just how it is for me. It's how I was raised and it's how I think it should be."

"Oh." He doesn't say anything more, just turns a little and looks down the street. When he turns back, he's grinning again, "So...we don't have to talk about the whole club thing then, right?"

"Noooo." I shake my hands in front of me and laugh too. "We're good."

15 Her

"Hey, wake up. This party is for you, you know?" Cathy is shaking my leg. I look at my watch, it's only 10:30 but I'm falling asleep on her sofa.

I sit up more. "Sorry. I've been asleep by 11:00 lately." I rub my eyes and yawn. "Sorry." I laugh. "Thanks for putting this together." I hug Cathy again.

"No problem. I'm glad to celebrate with my fabulous sister-in-law. Now get up and mingle." She pushes me towards my friends.

I've looked forward to tonight all week. The stress of getting so much work done in such a short period of time, both for me and Max, has been putting a strain on the happiness of seeing all the details come together. I'd hoped that this party would help me to relax again.

I've hardly seen Max all week. *I've seen Jeff more than him.* He comes home late and goes straight to his den to keep working, closing the door and only coming out to tell me to go to bed.

Tonight he was attentive. *Sort of.* I rub my hands down my butt quickly. He gave me one of his maintenance spankings before leaving for his party. I blush just thinking about it. But we didn't have sex like usual. He just rushed out the door afterwards. *Can't be late!*

I take a deep breath and try to enjoy the party again. But I keep looking at my phone wondering if Max will text or call me.

16 Him

"Oh. You're *finally* home?!" She sits up and turns on the bedside lamp. I can tell that she hasn't been asleep. I stand next to the bed and reach for her hair. She looks so pretty with her pout and bed-head, but I frown seeing that she's wearing my t-shirt. And she pulls her head away from my hand slightly.

"Lose the shirt, Lucy. You know better." I head towards the bathroom.

She yells after me, "Why do you smell like cheap perfume, Max?!"

I turn around slowly. She's still sitting in the bed with the shirt on, her eyes narrowed, arms crossed.

"I'm giving you to the count of three to take that shirt off and wipe that look off your face, little girl. One, two," She quickly whips the shirt off and throws it towards my feet on the first count. But she's only narrowed her eyes more. I take one step towards her with, "Three," and she lowers her head, covering her face with her hands.

I head into the bathroom again. I've had to pee since leaving the party; I've had too many beers. I sniff my shirt as I take it off. *She's right*. All the strippers had a lot of perfume and glitter. It got everywhere. I take off all my clothes and get in the shower.

It's not long before Lucy comes in. She stands a little away from the shower door, watching me. I open the door and steam avalanches out. "Come here."

She doesn't move, just keeps looking at me for a moment. "Why do you smell like cheap perfume?" She doesn't have the narrowed look anymore, more of a pout. It's her tone that peaks my anger. *Petulant*.

"Get your ass in here. Now." She jumps, the words reverberating on the tile, adding volume to go along with my edge. She's quick to step into the steam, but stays on the edge.

I grab her arm and yank her towards me, her feet slip on the wet tiles. I have a firm grip on her arm though. She isn't going anywhere. I shove her face first against the wall and slap her wet ass hard on her left cheek. She cries out and tries to twist around, but I have her firmly pinned.

I see a few light pink marks from the spanking earlier. I aim my next three swats on these, pressing hard with my hand, pushing her hips into the tile. The water adds to the sting on my hand, so I know it's adding heat to her ass too. I hit three more times on the same spot, a nice red collage of my handprint forms. I finally let go of her arm, but she stays against the wall, crying softly.

I wait for her to calm a little before saying anything, but she speaks up, still with her face to the wall. "And I suppose you're just going to send me to bed now..."

I smile. She can't see me, her face is buried in her wet hair, forehead firmly against the wall. *So my little girl needs a little attention.*

I get rid of any trace of smile in my voice. "Turn around, Lucy."

She twists, her hair wrapping across her face and shoulders, her arms hugging around her waist. Her nipples are red from rubbing against the tiles. The petulant pout is gone. I put my arms out and she's instantly pressing against my chest, her arms around my waist. The water runs over us.

But she asks again, quieter, without a tone, "Why did you smell like that?"

"Because Dan had strippers, lots of them." I laugh remembering how her brother had a lap dance from almost all of them. *His wife is definitely going to be asking some questions tonight.*

She jerks her head up and tries to push out of my arms, but I hold her in place. "And you think that's funny? What if *I* had strippers at my party? Would you think *that* was funny?"

I grab her arm again and twist her back to face the wall. I deliver five quick, hard swats to the reddest part of her cheek. She's crying out and dancing against the wall, but I keep her pressed to it. "Don't try my patience, little girl." I take a deep breath. "Are you done mouthing off?"

She only mumbles what sounds like, "Yes, Sir." So I spank her three more times, getting a louder response with each one.

"Stay facing the wall." I take a few deep breaths, pushing the water back through my hair. Her cheek is a deep purple red now. Her cries have melted into shakes.

I put my hands on her shoulders and turn her into my chest again, turning the water off. I lead us out of the shower and wrap a towel around her first. She doesn't dry off, just stands with it wrapped around herself, her hair a waterfall. I wrap my towel around my waist and put my arms around her to warm her up. I move her towel up and rub her hair with it. She finally takes it from me and wipes herself dry.

I walk us back into the bedroom, allowing her to keep the towel wrapped around her arms. "Now. Do you want to tell me what has you so upset tonight?"

Her pout is back, but she's trying to hide it. "I haven't seen you all week and you come home smelling like cheap sex. *That's* what I'm upset about."

She must be upset, because she's pushing every limit and she knows it. She hasn't looked up, cowering in the towel, but she still didn't manage to keep the insolence out of her voice in the end. "Try again." I don't hold back any anger.

She cowers more, but takes a deep shaky breath, tilting only her eyes up to me, "I've missed you. And I don't like that you had strippers at your party."

I relax a little. "That was better." I put my arms around her. "I didn't *have* any strippers, baby. They were there, but I didn't have any lap dances or anything else. I wouldn't even let them pour shots for me."

"You swear?" She's snuggling into my chest with her cheek.

"I would never disrespect you like that, Lucy." She pushes herself into me more. "And I've missed you too." I pull her face up to mine and kiss her open mouth.

I take the towel from her and toss it towards the closet. She takes mine off me without waiting and tosses it too, smiling her delicious wicked grin at me.

"On the bed." She quickly jumps on it, on her knees facing me. "Lay down, legs spread wide." She does. I know she feels self-conscious, exposed and open to me like this. I sit next to her. She reaches for my thickened cock, "No, hands behind your head." She does, with a small cute pout.

I put my hands around her throat, squeezing slightly. Her eyes flash fear for only a second before she relaxes. I rub my hands across her chest, pinching both nipples playfully, before running my fingernails down her stomach. She giggles and twitches, but stops when I pull her pussy hair. I give it a good tug. Her eyes widen with shock. I grin.

I get on the bed, between her legs, squeezing her thighs painfully for a moment. I slowly lower my face to her pussy. Her eyes are wide with shock again. I've never licked her. I always make her suck me. *But my little girl needs my attention.*

I grin again, keeping my eyes on hers. Her breathing is heavier now. I put my mouth to her and push her lips open with my tongue. She forgets her self-consciousness and starts to moan loudly. I watch as her head pushes back and her mouth opens a little. *Good girl.*

I close my eyes and concentrate on her. I explore her with the tip of my tongue, the soft outline of her lips, the hard knob of her clit, the heat of her inside, the deeper opening tightening and pushing against me, layers of sweet petals. *All mine.*

I flatten my tongue and explore again, slowly, a dessert I want to enjoy devouring. I open my eyes and her head is shaking side to side; her deep moans are trapped behind her lips. I watch as she gasps, my flattened tongue pressed into her clit, rubbing up and down fast. My teeth nibble her swollen clit with quick beaver jabs; her gasp is a sharp intake. Her stomach flutters with tiny orgasms and long moans. I press her clit again with my flat tongue and taste her warm wetness. She raises her upper body off the bed, and lets out a high-pitched moan. I lift my face and smile at her, kissing her thighs and wiping her come off my lips.

"Good girl."

I sit up and position myself between her legs and lower my body onto her, crushing her a little before raising up on my hands. Her legs wrap around my legs, feet anchoring her to me. I slide right in and moan at the swollen tightness. She whimpers under me, head pushed back into her hands. I slide, slow and steady, deep and long, pulling my cock all the way out and back in, pushing against the roof of her pussy, dragging against her clit. She pulls her hips up with her legs to meet my thrusts. I explode deep inside her, feeling her lips fluttering on me; her cry is a deep long moan in my ear.

With my face buried in her hair, "God, I love you." She giggles in response, pushing me out of her.

17 Her

"I'm really gonna miss you, Lucy-Goose!" Kevin is already a little tipsy. *For all his claims of being a party-boy, he can't hold his liquor at all.* I'm standing next to his chair, but it takes all my strength to push his upper body back into his seat.

"I'm not going anywhere. We *can* hang out, ya know." He wraps his arms around my waist and hugs my side to him. Rosa puts another carafe of wine in front of him and smiles at me. He lets go and pours himself some more. It's not Wednesday, but I couldn't imagine having my going away party anywhere else besides Romona's.

I move down the table to stand in between Laura and Tracy. They both put their arms around my hips. Tracy picks up her glass and cheers me, "This is kinda nice. Let's have a Lucy-party every weekend from now on."

I reach over and grab my almost empty glass from the other side of the table, "Well, next week is the big one."

"Where are you going on your honeymoon?" All three of our faces turn to Cruela, sitting next to my empty chair. I can't believe it, but she was actually nice to me all day. She even complimented me on my final report of Rich's team and the recommendations for training that I made going forward for any new hires.

"Um...I don't know. Max wants it to be a surprise." Laura smiles up at me. She knows the underlying message here.

"That's so nice. My first husband...he was full of surprises." She smiles, but there's a sadness behind it. I know he died in a skiing accident. We never talked about it, of course, but everyone knew. No one knows much about her current husband, other than he doesn't work. She doesn't bring him to any of the company events.

"Rich! Glad you could make it." Catherine puts her hand up to wave.

I turn around slowly. I didn't invite him. *Actually, I didn't invite most of these people.* I was surprised at the number that showed up. Rosa just kept bringing out more platters of food and wine for everyone. She told me before we sat down that Max is taking care of the bill.

Rich steps closer to me and I take a step back into Laura's arm more. "I wouldn't miss this send off." He reaches for my arm and I do a little twirl around Laura to sit down in the vacated chair next to her before he can touch me. She's frowning and questioning me with her look, but I just shake my head.

I still haven't told her how upset Max was about Rich touching me at the party. We've talked more over the last two weeks about my relationship with Max, but I've not told her about his spanking me yet.

Rich goes around the other side of the table and takes my seat next to Catherine. He keeps looking at me with a sad smile, but doesn't say anything. He already confronted me earlier today, saying that he would miss me. But we both knew he was saying more than that. I ignored it then and I'm ignoring it now.

"Max." I hear Rosa calling out his name from outside the back room and turn to see his smiling face as he enters. His smile falters for a moment when he sees Rich sitting opposite me, but he walks into the room slowly.

Everyone's congratulating him as he walks past. Kevin gets up wobbly and puts his hand on his chest and walks with him to my chair. "Wow. You are a beefcake. Damn girl!" He high-fives my shoulder, not noticing that I didn't raise my hand. He wobbles back to his chair and everyone laughs.

Max leans over and takes my chin, lifting my head even more to his and kissing my cheek. But I can see that his eyes are on Rich the whole time. "You having fun?"

"Yes, Si..." He grins that my response would be automatic to his only slightly edged voice.

Rosa comes over with a glass of wine for Max and stays to talk to him. He's offered to take a look at her lease for her, no charge. He keeps his hand on the back of my chair though.

Catherine reaches across the table and grabs for my hand with both of hers. "You've been such a big help, Lucy." She's drunk. *Wow. When did she get drunk*? We've been here for a while already, but I don't remember her drinking that much. "Rich, hasn't she been a big help?"

He puts his hand over Catherine's, covering both of ours, "Yes." He looks at me with such a mix of emotions. He just got here, but he's obviously been drinking as well. "I have greatly appreciated your help these two weeks, Lucy. And I *will* miss you." I pull my hand from under theirs.

"I'll miss working with all of you, too." I say this loudly, wanting Max to hear, but not looking up at him. I know he's paying attention despite the contract chatter he's having with Rosa behind me.

Laura puts her arm around my shoulder and pulls me towards her, "You won't miss me, cuz we're going to go to lunch and happy hours and here all the time still. Right?"

Tracy leans over her and grips my shoulder, pushing and pulling, "Yeah. All the time!" I only laugh in response, still shaken and pulled with them.

Rosa leaves and Max turns to face the table. And to my horror, Rich gets up and stretches his hand out to him. "Congratulations. You're a *very* lucky man."

Max takes his hand and shakes it once, hard, "I know." He puts his hand possessively on my shoulder and squeezes gently. When he looks down to me, I don't look away. I just smile up at him, hoping that this won't turn into an angry night. "We should get going, baby. Lots to do tomorrow."

"Oh...no...stay!" Tracy is play pouting and reaches out to push Max. He doesn't move, only laughs lightly.

"Sorry. Party's over." But he sounds light, happy. I get up when he pulls my chair and he pulls me close for a kiss. Laura clangs her glass and several people hoot. He kisses me once more before letting me go.

I hug a couple of people on the way out. Catherine and Kevin are both wobbly and give me a joined hug. I laugh having to push them off. Rich doesn't get up. He only gives me a half-smile when I wave to the room.

18 Him

"Are you going to miss working there, baby?" I kiss the top of Lucy's head, still warm from sex. She snuggles into my side more, her hand rubbing gently across my nipples.

"I don't know...maybe..."

"You'll miss seeing your friends is all." She nods and kisses my chest. "But you'll still see them." I rub her curls, enjoying the softness against my hand. Softness is in everything about her...her lips, hair, skin, how she looks at me, her voice, her laugh. I fell in love with her softness first.

"I know that we've both been busy. *I've* been working a lot the past few weeks." She nods a little harder. "But I promise that it won't always be this way. Being with you, making time for us, that's also my job, ya know..." She looks up and strokes my cheek, smiling at this. "And knowing that you're home, taking care of everything I need as my wife, will make me very happy." I kiss her forehead, still raised to me. "You will have chores and more rules. You'll be busy."

She swallows, but keeps her face turned up, "What kind of chores? You make it sound like I'm a child who has to keep her room clean..." She's smiling self-consciously at this.

"Well. Cleaning the apartment *will* be one chore. I have a cleaning service, but I've cancelled them starting the week we're back from our honeymoon." She looks around the room; it's a large apartment and I have it kept immaculately clean. She swallows again. "And keeping my work and social schedule will also be a chore. I told you that I have a lot of events. It takes some juggling to make it all work. And I'll be home for lunch each day. I'll have a list for you." She looks a little worried, but nods slightly. I lift her chin and kiss her soft mouth. "Get some sleep."

She snuggles back obediently into my arms and whispers, "I love you," into my chest.

"I love you, too, baby." I kiss her head again.

19 Her

I take a deep breath. *Today's the day*. The double doors open before me and the first thing I see, the first thing I *smell* is all the flowers. Gardenias, Magnolias, Orchids all greet me. *All my favorites*. They're everywhere, draping the aisle, hanging from the high tent roof, off the large chandeliers, even full-grown trees have lights woven into everything. It's a dream of flowers and sparkling lights.

"Here we go," Dad squeezes my hand on his arm and takes the first step down the aisle.

Max waits at the end with a big smile. His hands are at his sides, shoulders squared, coal black tux fitted to his body. I can see that he's taking deep breaths though; his chest pulls at the shirt buttons. I smile knowing he's nervous too.

The aisle isn't long, but it's covered in petals. I pass our friends and families in white chairs in rows draped in flowered garland. I'm stunned, hardly seeing faces, only Max's when I look again where I'm heading. I pass the last row and see both our moms crying into tissues.

Dad puts my hand in Max's and kisses my cheek. Max pulls me to him and his smile broadens even more. He leans in, but doesn't kiss me. "You are *beautiful*." I blush and feel my eyes tearing too. I blink these away.

I'm so dazed, I hold onto Max's hand for support. The words of our wedding buzz by me. I only hear and see Max, *his* strong profile, *his* big smile, *his* steady hands as he takes mine and places the simple band on the tip of my finger.

"I, Maximilian Drake Traeger, take you, Lucy, to be my lawfully wedded wife. To have and to hold, to love and to care for, to shelter and to lead until death do us part." The ring feels cool as it slips on me. I'm shaking as I turn to get the simple band I have for Max. Both share the engraving, "Always."

"I, Lucy..." my voice shakes and I stop to take a deep breath and swallow. Everyone laughs a little, but Max only squeezes my hand and nods encouragingly at me, "I, Lucy Elizabeth Shannon, take you, Max, to be my lawfully wedded husband. To have and to hold, to love and to care for, to please and to obey until death do us part."

I can hear the shifting in seats at our vows. I knew when Max told me what I was to say that there would be some raised eyebrows from our guests. I only see Max though. He's so proud, his eyes are even shining with unshed tears. I put my left hand on his cheek and smile serenely. I've never been more at peace and happy, all my shaking gone. He takes my hand and kisses my palm. The electric current runs down my stomach as always.

"I now pronounce you man and wife. You may kiss your bride." Max grabs me, lifting me off the ground and I giggle, my hands around his shoulders, our kiss is more a smashing of our smiles.

"I am pleased to present Mr. and Mrs. Max Traeger."

Everyone stands and claps. *And just like that, I'm married*!

20 Him

"Mr. Traeger, we're ready to serve whenever you are."

"Thank you, Stephen." I turn to look for Lucy. She's been surrounded by friends and family, circulating as much as the trays of hors d'oeuvre and drinks around the restaurant.

She was swept out of my arms the moment we moved everyone into the restaurant side of the reception. I move into the circle surrounding her now. Her grandmother is holding her left hand with her mom, Aunt Emma, and Cathy standing at her side. "Did I hear your vows right? They sounded like the ones I had to say to your PopPop when we married?" Lucy smiles; I interrupt her reply though.

"Lucy...we're ready to open the doors for dinner, baby." She takes her hand back and puts it in mine.

The staff have been busy rearranging the tented patio space from rows of chairs to tables for dinner, adding even more flowers with centerpieces. I stand with my arm around Lucy in front of the double doors.

I wait for a few people to notice us, then a general quieting down and turning in our direction. "Lucy and I would like to thank all of our family and friends for being here to celebrate our marriage. Chef David has put together a menu tonight that I am sure will be delicious." I gesture with my hand to the white-jacketed man standing off to my left, he bows his head dramatically. "Please join us for dinner."

The doors open and Lucy takes a deep breath in. "Is it what you dreamt of, baby?"

She smiles, tears forming again, and squeezes my arm with her other hand, "Yes. Thank you, Max!" The lights are lowered, but more candles create a warm glow everywhere. The fragrance from the flowers intermingles with the mouth-watering scent from the kitchen. *It's intoxicating.*

I lead Lucy through the tables to the center, a small table for us is placed right under the large chandelier. She takes her seat and wipes her eyes. "I still can't believe you were able to do all of this."

"All for you, my wife."

"Tonight has been beautiful, Max." Mom is hugging us both. Since dinner, I haven't let Lucy out of my reach except to let her dance with her dad and brother. "And, Lucy, you are the most beautiful bride I've ever seen!" She kisses Lucy's cheek. "I'm so proud to call you my daughter."

"I think my face is raw from smiling, blushing at compliments and being kissed all night."

I tell her for the third time tonight, "You are stunning, Lucy." She blushes again and puts her face against my arm.

Jake and Dad come over to stand next to Mom, "Can I steal her away for a dance?" Jake has his hand out to Lucy, but he's looking at me. That strange look is back on his face. *I'm going to have to ask him what that's about.* I nod towards Lucy and she puts her hand delicately into his.

He pulls her onto the dance floor and turns so his back is to us. The small band is playing only soft and slow music, background really. I wanted our reception to stay more sophisticated than rowdy party. I've invited a lot of the firm's and my own important clients tonight.

Seeing Jake with Lucy, though, I'm wishing for music that wouldn't have them dancing so close. But I shake my head and get a grip...*it's just Jake.*

"Dad, how bout we see to Councilman Riley's need for good scotch and bad cigars." He claps me on the back and we lead Mom towards a table of men all laughing loudly in the corner.

21 Her

"You *do* make a beautiful bride, Lucy." Jake leans in, his lips just brushing my temple as he says this. His hand is low on my back, fingers grazing my skin where the dress dips.

I blush and say a small, "Thank you." I'm not used to having so many compliments. Jake's closeness is making me nervous; his touch on my back tickles almost. I can't see Max over his shoulders and Jake keeps us dancing in a tight spot, hardly moving.

"Your vow...to please and *obey* my brother...caused quite a stir."

"I know." I laugh lightly. "Everyone's been asking me about it all night."

"And what have you answered?"

I have to remind myself that this isn't Max. Looking up into Jake's emerald green eyes, he sounds so much like him, "I said that Max is a very traditional man and he wanted traditional wedding vows."

He laughs, "Well...that's sidestepping it a little, don't you think?"

"No...Maybe...but it's none of their business anyway." I'm feeling a little raw from more than blushing.

"And now you'll be his very traditional wifey?" I look up to see if he's mocking me, but his smile is still sweet.

"Yes."

Jake doesn't say anything for a while, but moves us around a little more on the dance floor. People I don't know, Max's guests, keep smiling at me and I give little nods, embarrassed. He's introduced me all night to these important people. My small group of college friends and co-workers seems out of place, staying in a corner by the bar. *But everyone seems to be having a good time at least.*

"I've never seen Max as happy as he is with you." I'm startled to hear Jake's voice in my ear again, an intimate whisper, "Do you think I'll find that, Lucy?"

"I think...if you want to you will..." I don't know why his crooked smile is making me uncomfortable again, like I shouldn't be this close to him.

"I want to find what Max has with you."

I take the opportunity to joke, trying to lighten the tension I'm feeling, "Oh...now *you* want a traditional wifey, too, Jake?" His relationship with Julia was the opposite of what Max has with me.

"...Yes."

His smile is still crooked, relaxed, but his eyes are narrowed, searching. I'm surprised by his answer, "But...weren't you the one that wanted to warn me away from Max?"

"I didn't want you to get hurt." I don't answer, only look down. "But I can see that you're happy with him. And, Lucy..." He waits until I raise my eyes to him, "I can see that you accept him...just the way he is. You accept how we were raised. You're willing to live under his rules, just how he wants..." I only nod. "You've given me the hope to think that...well, that what I've wanted...that I could find that same acceptance."

We've almost stopped moving and I realize that I'm staring into his eyes. I lower my head quickly, "I'm glad for you, Jake. You deserve to be happy." I look up at him again and see Max heading towards us, but I keep Jake's stare, "I hope you find what you're looking for, too." He kisses the top of my head, a feather of a kiss against my hair, before dropping his arms and turning to Max.

"Your bride is a wonderful dancer, Max." He claps his brother on the shoulder and walks away.

Max looks from one to the other of us with a questioning look, before taking my hand and leading me towards a table of his important guests again.

"Did you have the wedding of *your* dreams?" We're walking hand-in-hand to our hotel. It's only a few blocks from the restaurant and the night air feels nice after the enclosed space.

He smiles and stops me, pulling me hard into his chest. "Yes. I have the *wife* of my dreams." Max kisses me hard, pulling me on to my tip-toes even more than my heels do. "I had a lot of questions about our vows..." He's grinning. I know he's pleased.

"Oh...probably not as many as *I* had!" I laugh.

"No...Probably not. But I heard you did just fine."

"And who did you hear that from?" I'm smiling up at his huge grin. *My handsome husband.* I look at the rings on my finger again. He kisses my forehead and releases his grip to continue walking.

"My dad. Jake." I expected him to say his mom. She kept checking in with me all night to see if I was doing all right.

"The funniest comments I got tonight were from Stephie and Becca. Something along the lines of, they thought you were into old-school kink not that you were *that* old-school."

"Mike said something similar to me." He laughs and puts his arm around me.

"The most serious were from my family and friends."

"I'm sure Tracy had a few choice words for me..."

"Oh, you could say that!" I laugh. "Cathy, my mom and aunt were pretty shocked, too. My dad actually came over and rescued me once during their questioning."

"Well...I assume you were honest in answering them..." He looks a little sternly at me, waiting to open the hotel door until I've answered him.

"...I was..." I say this shyly though. I wasn't as blunt as Max was to some of his clients and family. He told one man, a politician I think, that I was going to be his very obedient wife and that was just the way he liked it. I kept catching the man looking like he was undressing me every time I looked in his direction after that.

"Good girl." He opens the door and we head to the elevators.

22 Him

I stand Lucy back up and close the door to our suite. She doesn't move, just waits for me. "I've looked forward to carrying you across this threshold all night." I grab her in my arms again and run my fingers down her back to the end of the dress.

"You're beautiful. But this is definitely not the dress I thought I'd see you in today..." *How does she manage to blush so easily after a night of blushing at everyone's compliments and comments?*

"But you like it?" She's been nervous about what I would think.

"Yes..."

"Your choices were nice...but...well..."

"I didn't see any of the dresses. I only stressed that you be modest and covered up, nothing strapless."

"I'm covered!" I run my fingertips across her lower back, she blushes again, "*Mostly* covered...."

"Well...at least this doesn't look like it'll be difficult to get you out of..."

"Noooo." She laughs her sweet, high giggle, "I've had to stand very tall with my shoulders back all night to keep it up."

"I like you with good posture. A new rule." She pouts slightly at my grin. "For choosing a dress that every man there pictured falling off of you." I pull the dress gently off her shoulders and it drops quickly, exposing just the top of her nipples. Her blush runs further down.

I pull first one sleeve off, then the next. The dress drops to the floor, revealing only a tiny white thong underneath. I help her step out of this to the side. "Keep the heels on." She smiles wickedly at me.

I walk her by the hand to the bed.

I undo my tie and Lucy pushes the shoulders of my jacket back. I pull it off. I yank my shirt out of my pants quickly and she is already unbuttoning the top buttons; we meet down the middle. She kisses my chest, running her tongue across my skin, biting with tiny teeth marks. I smile. *My eager girl.*

I drop my pants and my cock pokes at the top of my boxers. I've been hard since watching her walk down the aisle. It was her sweet smile and submissive looks down; really, it was her vows in front of everyone.

Hell, I've been hard since this morning, picturing her tonight. And she's exactly how I imagined. Her smile is sweet with a little edge of daring. She tempts me to take her rough. But I want tonight to be gentle for her. *Well, a little gentle anyway...*

I grab her shoulders roughly and she cries out as I toss her onto the bed. She's laughing though as she lands, bouncing.

"Come here, *wife*." I stand near the edge of the bed. She knows this is one of my favorite positions. I can get into her so deep, holding her against me. She moves so her legs fall over the side of the bed, her pussy pushed past the edge. I push my boxers off and move closer to her.

"Put your legs up on my shoulders." She grins. I grab her ankles as her heels delicately point up to the ceiling. I bend a little to kiss her right thigh, running my stubble and lips up and down. She giggles.

I stop on my lips' travel back up, "I shouldn't have to tell you where to put your hands, baby." She quickly moves them behind her head. I smile. Her obedience makes my cock even harder. "Good girl." I pull her legs up tight against my chest, bending forward into her.

Pushing my cock down with my hand, I place the tip into her, "You are my good girl, aren't you?" I push in just an inch.

She moans, "Yes, Sir." She opens her eyes again, "Please. I need you..." Her voice, her smile, she licks her lips, it's all so sweet.

I can barely hold my lust back. I jackhammer into her with all of my strength, all of my thick stiff cock. It's an animal need, to stick my cock between her legs, to tear her moans from her, to remove all false sense of civilized love. I want to bring her face to face with the truth. She married an animal. I will have her. *So much for being gentle.*

I push into her, pinning her legs against me, holding her ankles painfully, lifting her lower body onto my thrusts. Her squeals and cries only make me fuck her harder, faster. I don't care if this is hurting her, her tiny cries only make me harder, stopping me from coming, pumping me more full of lust for her.

Her moans mingle with whimpers and I'm lost, I shoot into her with my last thrust. She shudders and rocks in my hands, her legs twitching against me. I wait for her last movements, before lowering her legs onto the floor.

"I don't think I can get up," Lucy smiles at me from the bed.

I feel a little lightheaded myself. I put my hand out and pull her up to stand next to me. Even in heels, she's tiny. Her nipples are hard and brush against me as she moves. It's only a tickle, a charge, a whip to my heated skin.

She turns to move towards the bathroom, but I grab her arm. I'm getting hard again. "Going somewhere?" I watch as her stomach flutters with a quick breath in. Her nipples stay hard and her eyes go soft once more.

"No, Sir." She responds so quickly. *It'll be her undoing tonight.*

I know that I have to have all of her, the one part of her I haven't claimed yet. Her look of fear is only a flutter in response to the change in my grin. "Lose the heels and get back on the bed."

"On your knees." I watch as she rolls over and pulls herself up to her hands and knees. Her hair falls to the side and she looks back at me. I know she thinks I'm going to spank her. She has one coming.

"I'm not going to spank you, little girl." And she frowns. I want to kiss her frown, that she wanted a spanking tonight. I have another punishment in mind. "But I *am* going to hurt your ass."

Her quickly changing expression is almost enough to make me laugh and lose my hard on. But her sole plea has me rock hard, "Please...no." She hasn't moved, she knows it would be no use. But her eyes are wide with fear and pleading.

"You are my *wife*. My *property*. And I'm claiming *all* of you tonight, little girl."

She lowers her head, her hair veils pools onto the bed. A shudder runs up her back. A tiny, "Yes, Sir," emerges from her forest of curls, but she keeps her head down.

I should relent. I should say that her willingness is enough for me. *I've never really been into it that much. But the thought of any part of her untouched by me... I can't have that. It's an animal thing.*

I get on the bed behind her, on my knees and she whimpers. She thinks I might stop if she begs with her little sounds. *She should know I won't.*

I put my hands gently on her hips and she automatically bolts forward in fear. I pull her roughly back to me with a growl. Her whimpers and whines excite me more. I take a few breaths to calm us both.

"Try to relax, baby." She takes one deep shattered breath in and out. *And God, how I love her*, she arches her back to me automatically.

I rub my right hand around her hip to find her clit, still swollen and wet. She gasps when I squeeze and rub her, she emits an animal moan to match mine as I enter her pussy. She's still dripping wet.

"You're not...?" The hope and relief in her voice should stop me, but I only feel harder at the thought of how much she doesn't want this.

"Just getting wet to make it a little easier on you, little girl." My voice is cruel. I like that she cries at this, her back and ass moving with a single sob of breath. But her pussy tells a different story, her clit swells even more. I know my cruelty excites her. Her mind may not want this, but her body needs to be claimed.

"Take a deep breath and hold it until I'm inside you." I pull out as she gulps air in. I keep my fingers on her clit and gently, slowly push into her ass. She cries out, a tearing of her lungs and ass. I stay half in her, waiting for her to calm her breathing again, only pressing her clit hard. I don't move my hips.

When she stops moving, I push in deeper and she only whimpers. I start rubbing her again and pull out slowly, halfway. Watching my cock pull at her hole, I have to breathe to stop from coming. *I want this to last. I want to take my time hurting her. I am an animal, a monster. And I love it.*

I push in hard and she screams out. But this only fuels my lust now. Her pussy drips on my fingers. I pull out further, slowly. She moans a long "No" sound, not quite saying it. But she stays in place, waiting.

"Tell me you want me."

She shakes her head, but cries out haltingly, "I want you."

I shove into her, the tight hole resists and pulls against me. Her scream melts quickly to a crying moan.

I pull out to the tip and push back in slowly, pushing hardest when I'm pressed against her ass. She bends forward but I yank her hip back into me. "If you move again, I'll take the belt to you and start over."

"I'm sorry!" She shakes and cries.

I keep pulling out and pushing in hard, slow. I shove two fingers into her swollen pussy and her pain is overwhelmed by her need to come. Her ass clenches and unclenches me and I'm unable to hold back. Her screams are overpowered by my animal howl above her as I fuck her ass hard, coming deep in her.

I pull out quickly and she collapses forward, mewing soft cries into the bed, shaking still. I get off her and go to the shower to clean up quickly. I start a bath for her.

She's standing when I return to the room. She's pale and shy. Her cheeks are stained with tears and makeup. Her hair is a mess. She won't meet my eyes. I took her to an animal place too. She came hard.

I put my arms out and she squeezes into me. "I started you a bath. Take your time, baby." I kiss her head and she walks slowly away. I know I hurt her. *I know all of her belongs to me.*

She stops at the door and turns, still not meeting my eyes though. "Thank you, Sir."

I let her walk way, but my cock is hardening again. I grin to myself, propping up in bed to wait for her. *We're not going to get much sleep tonight.*

23 Her

Curled up under a cashmere blanket, the sound of the jet engines and the soft flight attendant voices relaxes me, but I can't sleep. Max made me lie down on the sofa for a little bit, but I'm too wired. I want to pinch myself. He's been extravagant before, but this was beyond my wildest dreams.

Me, little corn-bred small town girl, in a private lux jet on my way to Rome. I've only been to Italy once before. *And not in this kind of style.* I look around at the muted tan tones and deep wood work of the plane. We've had non-stop offerings of food and drink. The bathroom has a shower and a large vase of orchids. *I think this jet is as big as my apartment was.* I snuggle into the deep sofa more, *I could get used to this.*

Max walks towards the back where I am and I quickly close my eyes. "You're not fooling me..." He rubs my head and sits on the sofa next to me.

I open one eye. "I tried to sleep, honest...I'm just too excited! I don't want to miss anything."

He laughs and moves so I can sit up next to him. "I'm excited to show you Italy too. This is my second favorite place in the world. Ron used to take us every summer for a family trip when Jake and I were younger." He pulls me onto his lap and looks at his watch. "We'll be landing in about forty minutes. Our hotel's on the north side of the city."

"What time will it be in Rome when we land?"

"We should get there a little before 5:30. Should give us enough time for an aperitivo and passeggiata before dinner." He tweaks my nose.

"I'm glad you picked Italy for our honeymoon. Thank you. For everything so far, Max." I kiss him, exploring with my tongue, tasting the strawberry still on his lips. I feel the familiar longing that this creates in us both. His cock hardens.

He holds me back, laughing. "You'll have to wait till we're in our room for that, baby."

"Okay...but your walk may need to be delayed, Mister."

"This bed is like a great big bag of fluffy goodness. I could stay in it all day. And look at this canopy...it's a cloud." I sit up, pulling a surrounding thick white curtain onto the bed.

"You better get up and get ready for dinner or you'll be enjoying a close up view of that bed post, little girl." He's smiling at me though. He pulls our luggage up onto the stands waiting for them. I jump out of bed and unzip mine next to him, still nude. He already took a shower and has his pants on.

"Where are we eating...fancy or casual?" My luggage is full of new skirts, tops, and dresses. Max insisted I visit Cassandra at Needless again and have her pick out appropriate things. I was irritated that she knew where we were going on our honeymoon, when I didn't. *But I do love all my new stuff.*

"Casual tonight I think. I haven't made any reservations. We'll just follow our noses to a good spot." He tweaks my nose again.

I stop smiling when I see him holding the belt. *I didn't know he'd packed it.* He smiles at the pout on my face. "Put this away and get ready quickly. I'll be downstairs having a drink." He kisses my cheek.

I put the belt in the closet and walk back slowly, still pouting. *I thought our honeymoon would be a spank-free time at least.* My butt still aches from last night.

I watch as he finishes dressing. A lightweight sports coat covers the light blue shirt and his strong shoulders. *My strong, handsome husband.*

"I'm starving. Get ready." He playfully smacks my hip. But he adds with a little sternness, "I'm giving you thirty minutes to be downstairs." He looks at his watch, "that's exactly 7:30."

"Yes, Sir." But I continue moving slowly towards the marble bathroom, watching him. Once I hear the door to our room close, though, I hurry to get ready. *This hotel smells like heaven. Even the toilet paper is scented.* I open every jar of fancy salts and soaps, choosing a rich amber colored one for a hot bath.

We had a gift of champagne, strawberries, mini-tarts, a candle, and chocolates waiting for us in the room. I finish my glass of champagne and nibble a little chocolate before running out the door.

In the small elevator, I adjust my boots and twist the hem of my dark blue dress around the right way. I didn't wash my hair, since it wouldn't be dry in time, just pulled it up in a loose knot. And I'm not wearing any makeup. I smile at myself in the mirrored panel. *Just the way Max likes me.*

I look at my watch. *Dammit*! I didn't adjust for the time change, but I can still tell that I have only minutes to find him downstairs. I tap my heel impatiently waiting for the elevator door to open.

Unfortunately, it opens on the second floor and an Italian couple gets on, slowly, squeezing together next to me. I smile, but I'm still tapping my foot. As soon as the doors open again, I dash out and look around. I can hear laughter coming from a bar area and head in that direction, hopeful.

I see Max sitting at the bar, drinking a glass of wine and laughing with another man and the bartender. He smiles at me and looks at his watch. I stop myself from looking at mine, still hopeful.

"Here is la mia bellissima moglie, Lucy." He introduces me to the man and the bartender. I smile as he puts his arm around me and kisses my cheek. "Right on time, baby." I breathe a sigh of relief.

Max continues talking to the man who turns out to be a small town official from Michigan named Ben. Max keeps his arm on me and gives me his seat, but he doesn't order me a drink of my own and only gives me a sip of his wine. The bartender asks with gestures and smiles if I'd like anything, but I look to Max to answer, just as he would like. He only shakes his head imperceptibly, so I decline with a small smile.

I've actually become very used to this aspect of our relationship. *He orders everything; I wait* for his pleasure. He gives me little gifts of drinks and food, what he thinks I'll like or knows I'll want. I blush thinking of how this makes me feel, how this makes me think. *Like a puppy waiting for a bone...a treat...from my Master.*

"Would you like a glass of wine, Lucy...I have a bottle open...?" Ben lifts his own glass and leans towards me.

I'm feeling bold, being far from home, so before Max can answer, "No, thank you. If my husband wants me to have anything, he'll order it for me." I look shyly up at Max who has his crooked grin up with a raised eyebrow. He lifts my chin slightly with his finger and kisses my cheek. I know I've pleased him and my pussy gets that jolt from my stomach again.

"You are a very lucky man, Max..." Ben stares at me though as he says this.

I was feeling bold and I don't like this man. Something about his overbearing, overly loud nature. *I know, don't judge a book.* But after interviewing thousands of people, I trust my instincts when it comes to quick judgments like this.

"Yes. I am. And we should get going. Lucy, I'll be right back, I'm going to drop the key with the front desk." He kisses my cheek again and walks away.

"So..." Ben smiles at me and leans in again. "Do you want that drink now that your *husband* isn't watching...?" He almost spills his glass sloshing it over my legs.

"No. No, thank you." I look towards the direction Max left. And this creep puts his hand on my knee. My instincts kick in and I slap his hand hard. "Get your hand off me!" I say this louder than I intended, the bartender is quickly over to our side again. But Ben just sits back and laughs at me.

Before Max, I probably would've handled that a little differently. I wouldn't have been so quick to show my anger at being pawed by a stranger. I would've tried to be politely firm, maybe gently pushed his hand off or moved my leg to lose it. I never liked overly friendly pushy men before Max, but now I see that I don't have to allow a man to get away with touching me like that. *I don't need to be polite to inappropriate strangers.*

Max returns and takes my hand while I stand. He leans over the bar and leaves an extra tip for the bartender with a nod. Before moving away though, he turns his head and says quietly, very close to Ben, "Touch my wife again and there might be a story about you being thrown into the Tiber in tomorrow's La Repubblica." Max doesn't move, but when Ben sits back more, he steps away.

When we're outside, I quickly turn to Max and put my hands on his chest, "You're not mad at me; you *can't* be mad at me?!"

He smiles and presses my hands against his chest. "No, baby, you did fine. That guy was just an asshole." He puts his arm around me and turns us onto the street to walk. "Let's head down the Via del Corso for a while and we'll find a place to eat on a side street."

"My feet are killing me. I don't think I could've walked another step today."

"Not even for another scoop of stracciatella?" He's laughing at me. We've had gelato at least once for the last seven days and I always get the same one.

"Not even for that."

The sun has set and the lights of the city shine back at us. The night air is warm enough that the restaurant's terrace is still candlelit and we can enjoy a drink outside before our reservation.

Max takes yet another picture of me, this time with the Dome lit behind me. "I can't help it. You're just so beautiful."

"So we've been under the Coliseum, under the Vatican, through Hadrian's, we've walked for hours and hours...what's on the agenda for tomorrow?" I don't even know how long we're staying; he won't tell me. I know that I have a lot of unworn clothes still, but I laugh realizing how much I've given to Max the past few days.

I haven't had a say in anything this entire trip. He's planned everything out, from private tours and cars, to where we eat. I asked to go back to a shop yesterday and he wouldn't let me. He didn't explain why, just told me no. And I didn't argue. *A test maybe? He's usually so indulgent of my wants and needs.*

He's shown me parts around Rome I didn't know existed. The tomb below the Vatican, the sacred mosaic there, where our feet followed the path of Popes. The exotic fountains of Villa d'Este where we enjoyed the best gelato outside the gates. An underground Osteria where the walls were covered by ancient graffiti. A warehouse of restored museum pieces where we were spoiled with awe by what few ever get to see. A private garden with rare sculptures of liquid beauty where we kissed at every turn. A cooking class with three Nonnas where we stuffed ourselves on plate after plate of pasta. *I think that one was more for him. He wants me to be a good cook.*

"*You* are going to pack us up tonight. We're heading to Capri tomorrow."

"Yeah. I've never been south of Rome. How are we getting there?" I'm excited to see a new area of Italy.

"That's enough questions, little girl. You'll pack us up when we get back to the hotel, we have an early departure tomorrow. *That* is all you need to know." He squeezes my arm and smiles smugly at me. I know he's enjoyed this total control. Since our wedding day, he's had absolute power over me. *And I've never seen Max happier.* I smile knowing that he's happy with how I submit to his control. *Making him happy makes me happier.*

24 Him

"I could get used to living on an island." I take another shot of the Faraglioni, still not tired of our view out to sea.

"I could get used to living on *this* island." Lucy laughs, stretching on the lounge chair, arms straight in the air, fingers wiggling. I snap another picture of her and she laughs harder.

In Rome, we ran around all day, down, up, around the Eternal City. Seeing everything again for the first time together. *I felt like a kid.* This leg of our honeymoon has been more relaxed. Our routine has been to do only one thing in the morning and spend the afternoon around our villa and pool. We've explored most of the island, rented a boat, hiked past the flimsy gate up the Via Krupp and through the Gardens, around the Villa Jovis, over the rooftops to Anacapri. But always back for an afternoon of swimming and lounging, fucking and napping.

The tourist season is ended here; the pace is slower. La Piazzetta is quieter, shop and restaurant owners stop to talk more, haggling anything. I negotiated the price for a lobster dinner with the owner of a restaurant last night; we were his last customers before closing up and heading to his vineyard on the mainland. He threw in the best fresh scampi I've ever had too. Of course, he sat and drank half our wine and charged us for the pleasure of his company. *But that was a part of the bargain.*

"I like the idea of you on an island..."

"Oh...why's that?" She's squinting up at me, her eyes brighter than the sea in the setting sun.

"I could keep you all to myself. You'd be trapped, only able to come and go as I please. I'd be your Caesar."

She laughs and reaches her hand out to me, "Don't you already have that power...without need of a sea?"

I kiss her hand. *This trip has been good for her.* The perfect start to our lives as man and wife. She won't be surprised when we're back home and I expect the same behavior. *She is on an island of my choosing, and I'll keep her there.*

I step back to the terrace wall. Waves lap the rocky beach below. "Come here." She gets up immediately and comes to me. *I love her lack of hesitation on this trip.*

I turn her to face the water and stand behind her, pushing her forward, placing her hands flat on the stone wall, looking out to the jutting fragments of rock. She doesn't resist. I hold the skirt of her dress up, exposing her nice round ass, the top of her pink frilly thong peeking out. She raises onto her tip-toes, just the way I like, arching herself to me.

"Do you know why I'm going to spank you, Lucy?"

"No, Sir." Still no hesitation. Only an added hunger lines her voice.

I run my hand up her leg and squeeze her right cheek hard, she breathes out slowly, staying on her toes. "Because I want to. Because I can." I smile. "Because I can't imagine a more perfect view than your bottom matching the reddening sky."

She swallows hard, "Thank you, Sir."

I slap her right cheek hard, pushing her forward, bending her elbows with the blow. A soft moan escapes her lips, but is made louder by the next slap to her left cheek. I alternate between them, right left right left right left, taking my time between each flat whack, pushing her forward each time, waiting for her to come back for more. She stays on her toes, only whimpering softly with the last one.

"Keep your dress up and stay facing the sea." I take her seat on the lounger and watch as the setting sun outlines my beautiful girl. Her skin glows against the darkening sky, my handprints match the sun's fingers stretching across the water. She stands with her shoulders back, the dress high around her waist, chin up.

When the last of the light dips into the water, "You may lower your dress and turn around."

Her smile is wicked. She starts to move towards me, but stops with a startled cry and her hand to her mouth. I turn in the seat and follow her stare. Up the hill to our right is another villa, with a terrace. A man in a light suit has been watching the sun set on Lucy too. I start to chuckle as Lucy runs into the living room.

As I stand to follow, the man raises his hand in a wave, a tipping of his non-existent hat to me. I smile and raise my hand to him.

"Lucy...you know better than to run away from me like that..." but the chuckle is still in my voice.

"Did you see? That man was watching us!" She's whispering like she could be overheard by someone in here.

"So what? That's no excuse for you leaving my side..." I try to put a little sternness into my voice, but fail miserably. *The look on her face is just too damn funny*. "Come here."

She moves into my arms and I kiss the top of her head. I walk us to the sofa and lie down, propping my head up on the arm. She watches as I undo my pants and pull my cock out. She's on her knees quickly and I breathe sharply in as she grabs my cock in both hands and puts her mouth around me in one movement.

Her lips tighten and relax, her tongue pushes and wraps as she raises her head and hands up and down my cock. She's learned how I like it. I yank her head back and my good girl whines, not at the pain, but at being forced to stop. "Get on me." She stands and drops her thong quickly. Putting her knees into the sofa, she lowers herself onto me. Just like I like, all the way down, her dress pools around us.

Hands behind her back, she slowly raises herself up and down. *She's gotten good at this.* Her legs are stronger from jogging.

I like watching her, head back, eyes almost closed, concentrating on her movements, squeezing me like I like. *But I like fucking with her too.* I grab the front of her dress and yank her towards me, stopping her from falling against me at the last second with my palm. Her hair blankets over us, her hands still behind her back. I push her with my palm and pull her with my other hand squeezing her tender ass. She continues to try to rock her hips against me more, but I'm controlling our movements now, pushing and pulling her faster.

I give one final push and she sits up, hair whipping to the side, I slap her exposed cheek hard and she cries out, eyes wide open, not moving her hips. I growl, "Don't stop," and keep my other hand on her ass, pulling her towards me. She moves her hips and I pull her into me deeper when she rocks away, slapping her cheek again.

Her eyes take on that look I can't get enough of, soft, yielding, wanting. She's told me that her fear of me makes her even hungrier for me, for my love. I continue slapping her with each quick pull forward and she keeps her chin up like I've taught her, squeezing and crying out. I yank her head back as she comes loudly, her body rocking against me, stealing the last of my own control with her spasms.

"Nic, I'll text you when we're ready to head back." He nods and drives off. I put my arm around Lucy and head towards the restaurant just off the square. She looks beautiful in a tight tan sweater and skirt, showing off her sandals from Anacapri. We walk by the busy tables on the cobblestones and the owner's wife welcomes us with hugs and air kisses. She says she held our favorite table for us and we show ourselves upstairs, to the balcony.

"Ah, hello." I stop and turn to the man sitting by himself at the table next to the balcony.

I frown for a moment, trying to place his face before I slowly smile. "Hello, neighbor." Lucy stands waiting next to her chair, she knows not to sit without me. But she can't see the man I'm talking to. "Lucy, come say hello." I see her flush as she stands at my side, recognizing the man who saw her spanking earlier.

"I was beginning to think that I was the only tourist left on the island." The man laughs, appraising Lucy up and down, before meeting my eyes again. "It's always nice to see other Americans on holiday." His accent has a hint of British, maybe London, but too muddled with a stronger New York accent. He puts out his hand and we shake, "Names Randolph Richards...a horrible joke I think from my British mum." He laughs at himself and his cheeks turn as rosy as Lucy's.

"I'm Max Traeger. This is my wife Lucy." She continues to only shrink next to my arm. In a voice that has her jumping, "Don't be rude, little girl."

"Hello." She says quietly, only raising her eyes for a moment.

"Charming." Randolph smiles at me. "Have you eaten here before? I only just arrived yesterday..."

"Yes. This has become our favorite spot." Something about how embarrassed Lucy is acting makes me want to embarrass her even more. I see his table is set for one. "Are you dining alone? Would you like to join us, Randolph?" I'm pleased to see the redness in Lucy's cheeks deepen. She puts her hand lightly on my arm, but doesn't say anything.

"I'd be delighted, Max. Oh..." He looks around for the waiter, but isn't getting anyone's attention.

I speak up, "Pasquale," the waiter stops in front of me and gives me a quick handshake and air kiss hello, "We'd like Mr. Richards here to join us for dinner. Please add a setting to our table." He moves quickly to make this happen and pulls the table out a little for Lucy to sit on the outside. She smiles a thanks to him, but continues to keep her eyes down.

The waiter hands Randolph and me a menu before walking away. "Don't you need to see a menu, Lucy, or do you already know what you want? Perhaps you can help me with a choice...?"

She looks to me to answer, actually pleads a little with her eyes. I grin, "You're being rude again, Lucy..." The hint of threat is obvious.

"...My husband orders for me..." She says this very quietly, but I'm proud to see that she keeps her chin up. "The mussels last night were very nice." But she hasn't looked at either of us. Her hands wring her napkin into a tight twist.

Randolph grins at me. He's probably in his 60's, with a portly belly more than started. I grin back. He seems to get the picture pretty quickly, "Your wife is very charming indeed, Max."

"Thank you. This is our honeymoon actually. And Lucy is still learning." I wink and he laughs out loud again.

"I believe I witnessed a lesson earlier tonight." His grin turns a little embarrassed. Lucy lowers her head and shrinks in her chair at this. "I'm afraid I have to apologize for *my* rudeness. I just couldn't take my eyes away."

"No...I should apologize. No one's been in that villa since we arrived. I should have checked first." I look at Lucy, her face is paled. I think she's holding her breath. "Lucy, sit up straight." She immediately does, but her eyes and chin stay down.

"We should celebrate your matrimonial bliss! Oh...what was his name?...Right...Pasquale. We need your finest Amarone...and you might as well bring two bottles to save yourself a trip." He pats his stomach and relaxes back into his seat, smiling from me to Lucy. "I don't think I've met a couple quite like you... Well, not since I was a boy anyway."

"The days when men were men...?" I laugh at using this phrase, but it probably suits his cowboy image of that era.

"Yes. And women were still treated like property...?" He wags his bushy brows at me with a little giggle.

Lucy squirms in her seat, looking at me sideways. I smile at her, taking her hand under the table. "Exactly."

Randolph giggles again and Lucy blushes more. "I find it very refreshing. No misunderstandings about who's who and what's what. Very refreshing."

Lucy finally stops looking so uncomfortable with the help of a second glass of wine and more of the spaghetti alle vongole she liked. He has her shyly giggling over a story of a couple he met last month in Venice, also on their honeymoon. Apparently Randolph had enjoyed cigars with the husband earlier in the night. But over dinner, the man kept spitting into his wine glass.

"And making the most horrible sound while doing so. It was drawing quite a bit of attention to our table. The wife only laughed and looked like he does this sort of thing all the time." I'm laughing picturing Randolph in the middle of a restaurant with these two. "Well...to put it delicately...the sight of the side of this man's wine glass was too much for the large meal I had enjoyed up to that point." He pauses dramatically to take another sip of wine. "I lost that divine meal on the floor of the restaurant!" He starts laughing harder, waving his hand in front of his red face.

"But what was worse," he interrupts himself with laughter again, "when I came back to the table, the waiters were clearing the floor, I was giving Euros to anyone with a hand out in retribution," he stops to laugh again, "and this sweet elderly couple was trying to get away from the mess. The *husband*...he's *still* spitting into his glass!" We're all three laughing hard now. "And this sweet elderly woman almost slips on the floor. What do you think the man had to say for himself?" He laughs too hard to tell us for a second, wiping at his eyes. "Yo, that'sa his tomato!" He does a perfect New Yorker and we're all holding our sides laughing.

"That's awful! Did you get out of there as quick as you could?"

Randolph continues laughing too hard to answer Lucy, "No...I ordered dessert." She laughs harder at this. He sobers enough to add, "I was hungry after all," and pats his middle.

She giggles more. "I wouldn't have given up dessert either."

"Well...with your permission...?" He looks to me; I nod, "I saw a few I'd like to try from here, but I can't possibly order all three just for me...you'll help me, won't you, Lucy?"

Lucy looks to me and smiles when I nod again. *She's getting used to her role in public.*

25 Her

"Hey."

"Yeah...you're home." Laura sounds excited to hear from me. I wasn't sure she'd pick up being a work day. "I know you didn't know how long you'd be gone..."

"We got back yesterday. I've been sleeping since."
Well...mostly sleeping anyway.

"Where'd you go?"

"We went to Italy. Rome and Capri. It was amazing, Laura."

"I am so jealous. I've always wanted to go. Did you take lots of pictures for me at least?"

"Max took a ton. I'll send you some." I look at the dining table, where my list of chores for the day sits. Downloading the pictures is #7. I was a little shocked yesterday to see the list waiting for me when we got home. Max put it there before he left for our wedding.

"So...how was it?" I giggle and she laughs, "That good, huh?"

I giggle more, "Yes!"

"Okay, details...and I don't mean about the ruins either."

"It's ten in the morning. Shouldn't you be in a meeting or something?" I laugh, but I miss seeing her around the office already.

"Good point. Okay, come for lunch then."

"I can't." I pause though on the rest. *I think I can say this to Laura...but only her. I could use one friend who understands exactly how things are for me anyway.* "I didn't get Max's permission..." This is what he expects of me. Saying it out loud, the opposing humiliation and pride, I feel a little giddy.

I had this reaction on our honeymoon. Acting so obviously submissive to Max around strangers, I felt a lot of humiliation. There were looks from people, comments. But I also felt this strange sense of pride. *I am his possession, his property. And I'm proud of that. I'm proud of how happy I make him.*

"Oh..." I wait to see what else Laura will say. We talked a lot before the wedding and at the reception she helped to smooth things over with Tracy about my vows, but I've never been this blunt with her. "Well...then check about tomorrow...or come to Romona's Wednesday?" She sounds fine. I let my breath out. I'm really going to have to get more details about that guy she dated in college.

"Okay. I'll let you know." *I can't believe how easy that was. I know I won't be having this conversation with Tracy.* "And thanks, Laura."

"No problem. I'll let Tracy know you're back too. She's been driving me crazy with the whole 'how could she be okay with not knowing how long she's going to be gone' shit. I'll tell her you're going to try to come Wednesday to shut her up."

I laugh. We hang up and I finish my coffee on the sofa. I smile thinking of my list, but I keep going back to yesterday instead of getting up.

Max carried me over the threshold again. And when he set me down, he said, "*This* is your island, Mrs. Traeger." Looking around the apartment now, *it's a nice island. I'll happily come and go just as Max pleases.*

And I better get going! I have to finish some items on his list before he comes home for lunch. And I have to log some distance at the gym in the journal Max gave me.

26 Him

I drop the plastic dish on the coffee table in front of her. She jumps and looks up at me before frowning down at it. I finish buttoning my shirt. Lunch and a quickie has been our routine.

"I've made an appointment for you tomorrow." She doesn't move just stares at me from the sofa, her legs bent under one of my t-shirts, arms crossed on her knees.

We've been back from Italy for two weeks and she's settled in nicely to the routine I've set for her. Each morning, I leave her a list of chores, each afternoon I come home for lunch to check her progress. I haven't let her leave the apartment except for a chore. And she hasn't questioned when I tell her no.

"What's the appointment? ...I'm not due for," she raises her eyes to the ceiling, thinking, "five months."

I cup her cheek. "Because this is your last month of using those." I move my eyes to the container on the table. "As soon as the doctor okay's it, we'll start trying."

"But." She stops herself quickly at the clenching of my jaw. "I mean..." she swallows, "You want to start having a family this soon...we've not even been married for a month?"

I ignore her question. "You'll also need to discuss any pre-natal care. I've left a book about planning for pregnancy on your side of the bed. It has a list of questions I'll expect answers to tomorrow. Read the first three chapters today before I'm home for dinner."

I turn to get my jacket and she jumps up to follow me. "Max...wait...shouldn't we..."

I turn around quickly and grin when she backs up, "Shouldn't we...what?"

"We...we should talk about this..." She swallows and moves one foot behind her, like she wants to back up more.

I close the distance between us quickly and shove her against the wall, my hand on her chest. "Who do you belong to?"

"I belong to you, Max." She answers without hesitation.

I move my hand down to her belly, gently, "Yes. You do. And you'll do exactly as you're told."

"Yes, Sir." Her stomach shakes against my hand with a long breath in and out.

"I want my child inside you, Lucy." The blue of her eyes swims in the tears not shed. I say in a low growl, close to her ear. "And when I spread your legs, I want you to pray each time for a baby." I pull back to look as two tears blink down her cheeks. I move my hand and wipe one away, kissing the other.

"Yes, Sir." She whispers against me.

I stay close, my voice almost a whisper too, "You gave up control of your body, baby. I thought you understood that."

"Yes, Sir." She pushes into my hand still on her cheek. *My sweet puppy.* "I do understand that. I'm sorry, Sir."

I stand back and take a step away from her. She waits with her hands almost behind her back. She instinctively tried to move them there when I shoved her. I smile and kiss her before leaving.

I know she's worried about getting pregnant. I'll ease her fears tonight when we discuss the book.

26 Her

I stand for a little longer in the same spot. I don't know for how long. I start to feel my feet going numb and finally push myself away from the wall.

In a daze, I walk into the bedroom. A thick pink and blue covered book waits for me. I sit next to it. I stare at it.

I don't know what I'm thinking. *Two trains, two tracks.*

I always wanted a child, children. Max and I talked about it once. He said three. I joked; said why not ten. He laughed; said he wasn't sure my little body could handle even one Traeger boy's big head.

I always assumed we'd have kids, try to have kids. After he proposed, I cried telling him that my mom miscarried so many times. Aunt Emma did too. I worry that it will happen that way for me. He said we'd deal with whatever happens together.

But today, he wasn't talking, he wasn't dealing!

An unfamiliar flutter of anger flies in my head. I try to shake it away.

It's too soon. I'm not ready.

I want to scream this at him. As loud as he likes to make my scream when he punishes me.

I laugh a little. *I could imagine what would happen if I ever dared to yell anything at him.*

I get up and walk to the bathroom, the mirrors reflect me back in multiples. I turn to the side, hand where Max's hand was. It's not anger I see. It's fear.

I'm afraid. I bow my head.

What if I couldn't give him something that he demanded? What if he couldn't control everything about my body? What would happen to us if I couldn't bend to his will no matter how hard I would try?

I shudder and put my arms around my middle, hugging myself. I'm not ready to face a possible darkened future. *A day that I couldn't give in to Max's needs.*

I shake my head a final time, close my eyes and breathe in normally. I let go of my waist and square my shoulders. But I keep my head down. I'll do whatever it takes to make Max happy. Whatever is in my power to do.

I want his child inside me too.

27 Him

I can hear Lucy laughing with her friends. I finally relented and let her go for their Wednesday night dinner. We celebrated our one month anniversary last weekend and she deserved a reward. Tonight is the first time I've let her off our island on her own.

I walk around the corner and stop. Jake's hand on my shoulder is quick to try to restrain me, but I'm frozen in place anyway.

I was supposed to work late, so Lucy's not expecting me. Jake came to the office, convincing me to go for dinner and drinks instead.

Lucy doesn't look up. Rich is sitting next to her. Close to her. She only mentioned her friends would be here tonight. *She knows I would never give her permission to go out with another man.*

And Rich has his hand over hers. He's smiling at her and talking to her and touching her. *My Lucy*.

"I'm going to kill him." It's more a rumble than words. Jake grips my shoulder more, but this won't stop me.

"Control yourself, brother." Jake's voice is only slightly less a growl than mine.

28 Her

As I'm pulling my hand back in my lap and trying to move away from Rich again, I see Max's face in the mirror above our table. *Oh my God.* Clearly he saw that. I swallow, not taking my eyes from Max's in reflection. He stopped at the small entrance to the back room. Jake is with him, also frozen, staring at me. I steal one quick glance at Jake and I see the same look. Shock. Disappointment. Anger. *The Traeger brothers, finally united.* I swallow again.

Laura's next to me. She sees my reaction and looks in the mirror. She stands up and turns to both men. I move in my chair to follow her, but don't stand, my back to Rich. I just sit with my offending hand in my lap. Rich and Tracy continue talking over the table; I can see he still has his hand on hers. I ignore them both. Rich puts his hand on my back and I jump forward, out of my chair, away from his touch.

But I see Jake's hand on Max's shoulder squeeze, his other hand grabbing his arm, holding him back, Laura still stands in between us. The wild look on Max's face is one I've not seen before. I'm too scared, too numb to hear what Laura says, but both men turn their eyes to her for a second. I take the opportunity to run away, out of the room.

I head outside. There's a garden room that isn't open anymore. The staff use it for smoking. No one is out here though. I can breathe fresh cool air and think. *How do I explain this to Max so he's not mad at me?*

It's Laura who finds me. "Max is waiting for you by the curb..." She moves my hair behind my shoulder and squeezes my arm. "You okay?"

"Yeah...I'll be fine..." She doesn't look convinced. I finally confide in her everything. "Max has a temper." She only nods and continues rubbing my arm. "He...he punishes me...when he's mad...when I've made him mad..." I don't look at her.

Finally, after she's not said anything for a while, I look up. "I told you that I had a boyfriend very much like Max...controlling...bad temper...jealous...I think I might know a little about what you're going through..."

I stare into her eyes for a long time. Not wanting to say more. Not wanting to leave. "What did you say to Max and Jake?"

"I told them that Rich just got here moments ago. And he's drunk. And you didn't do anything wrong." I squeeze her arm back.

"Thank you for saying that." I shudder and take a deep breath, looking down again. I can't stay here for long. *That would only upset Max more*. "Do you....do you think he believed you?" I hate sounding so pathetic, but I know the wrath that I'm facing.

"You'll be fine," she squeezes my arm again, "He loves you..."

I smile into hers, "Yeah...I know...I should go...will you tell Tracy...?" She nods. "Could you...could you get my purse and coat for me?" She nods again and heads back inside. I wait a moment before heading towards the door.

She hands me my things and hugs me quickly, "Call me tomorrow..."

I only nod and head out the door.

I see Jake waiting for me by the car. He looks about as angry as I expect Max to be. I stop a few steps away and just look at him. I plead with my eyes for him to understand. *Maybe he could help me with Max*.

"You've really messed up tonight..." He only indicates for me to get into the car. His voice matches the deep angry one Max uses when punishing me. I shudder before getting in. *He won't be any help*.

Max doesn't say anything when I sit next to him. Jake moves into the seat to my right and closes the door himself. I look at Jeff in the rearview mirror. *Not even he's looking at me*.

I stare at Max, but he's looking out the window as the car pulls away.

I look straight ahead. I can see both brothers in my peripheral vision. Their anger buoys in the small space.

Max finally looks forward and puts his hand on my knee. I can see Jake move his head slightly to look in our direction too.

"What were you doing with another man's hands on you again, Lucy?" He squeezes my leg painfully, but I don't move. "No...The *same* man you let touch you before?!" His voice fills the car. I shake, my leg going numb where he's still squeezing.

"I didn't..." but he doesn't let me finish.

"No. Shut up. Not a fucking word out of your mouth until we get home." He lets go of my leg and I have to stop myself from rubbing the red fingerprints, my hand shakes above my knee. I finally put my hand back in my lap. I don't look at anyone, just my hands. Max goes back to looking out the window.

I've never been more scared of him. After a moment, I steal a look at Jake, still hopeful that he might be able to help me. His jaw is as clenched, as set. He meets my sideways glance and gives me a shake of disapproval before turning his gaze out his window too. *I'm alone.*

I stop at the elevator, watching as Jake talks to Max on the curb. I can't see Max's face, but Jake's hasn't softened at all. Max finally comes in; he doesn't look at me, just puts his key card to the elevator and waits for me to get in.

I find the courage to ask, "What did Jake say?"

He grins at me, a frightful sight. His beautiful smile is twisted and angry. "He told me to take it easy on my wife." He laughs at this.

I shudder and shrink further against the wall of the elevator. I picture for a moment about not getting out when the doors open; I know this isn't an option.

Once inside the apartment, he closes the door quietly. I don't bother walking down the hall. I know what's coming next.

But he doesn't order me to undress or face the wall. He only walks down the hall. I hesitate a long time before following him.

He's moved onto the terrace. The fall breeze is chilling. He's poured himself a glass of scotch. I wait just by the terrace doors.

He takes a big gulp of his drink, holding it on the low wall. He doesn't turn around, only continues looking out at the city lights. "*Should* I go easy on you, Lucy?" His voice is steady. Not as I've heard from him before. *A mix of pain and anger that I've not known*?

"I..." I swallow my words. I want to plead for his forgiveness, his mercy, to explain that it's not my fault. But I know that if this were true, I wouldn't be in trouble. *I was guilty the moment I let Rich touch me that first time, in the office. Just a friendly gesture, nothing but a hand on my shoulder. But I was guilty of letting him think it was okay then.*

It's no excuse now that he was drunk and I didn't know he would be there. I take a deep breath and say nothing.

Max turns when I don't answer. He looks for a long time into my eyes. Searching for what I don't say. Finally, he nods. Only once, but it changes his whole expression. The pain is gone. In its place is pure anger. I shudder and take a step back.

20 Him

She steps backwards into the apartment, two, three steps. She turns away and moves faster into the room. But not fast enough.

I put my glass on the table and in two strides, I'm on her.

I grab her hair and yank her towards me. She cries out and her body snaps to me. I put my arm around her front, pinning her arms to her side, her body to my chest. Through gritted teeth, "Did I tell you to leave?"

She can only shake her head slightly more than her body is shaking against me. "No. I didn't. Just like I didn't tell you that you could be a *whore* tonight." I yank her hair back more, making her cry again. "But you *were* a whore, weren't you?"

She tries to shake her head, pulling without care against my hold on her hair. "No. Answer me. Say it, whore."

"I...I..." she sobs until I pull her hair again. "I was...whore." Her words choke on her sobs, her body folds against my arm despite the hold I have on her head.

I let her hair and body go, watching as she almost falls onto the sofa. She recovers and lands to face me, sitting with her hands bracing her sides. I stand over her.

"Say it again."

She shakes her head slightly, but repeats without a sob, "I was a whore." And I slap her. Hard enough to make her fall back against the sofa, putting her hand up to her face.

"Move your hand and say it again."

She stares at me with her hand up for a few blinks. I don't move. *She'll either do as she's told or be in more trouble. It's up to her.*

She slowly lowers her hand, shaking, and says it again. I smack her, just as hard; she's pushed off balance again.

My hand curls into a fist. It takes all my control to relax it again. *I can't hit her. I'd break her. But God help me. I want to.*

She lowers her hand and looks up at me. Waiting. Her eyes are brightened with fear. Her tits rise and fall quickly. But she sits completely open to me. Waiting for the pain she deserves.

"Stand up."

I don't move back, so she has to shakily stand inches from me. "You have to the count of three to undress." I count quickly while she undresses just as quickly.

She stands before me naked, her hands behind her back, trying to behave how I expect. I slap her left tit hard and grab her right arm before she falls back against the sofa. Holding her up, I continue to slap her tit several times. She keeps her hands behind her back, but cries out and begs with her eyes after a few slaps. But she doesn't speak or beg out loud.

I let her go and she falls back to the sofa, but bounces up to stand next to me again.

"Follow."

She moves quietly to follow me, with her arms loosely behind her back, her head bent forward.

I stop in front of the closet. "Get the belt."

Lucy opens the door and retrieves it, but holds it in front of her body, unsure where to put it. I take it from her gently. She hasn't tried to beg or persuade me not to be angry; it helps to hold my temper in check. *I know she understands how much she deserves to be punished.*

"I told you that if you ever let another man touch you, I'd beat you with this belt so badly you'd not be walking the next day." She nods with a heavy sob, not meeting my eyes. I lift her chin gently with the doubled belt to look into her eyes. Fear is only a small part of what I see. Her pleading and sadness match my anger. *I know that my Lucy is truly repentant.*

But it's not enough.

I need to see her tears.

I need to hear her screams.

30 Her

"Lie on the bed, face down." I crawl into the middle of the bed and lie flat. "Arms stretched above your head." I pull the cover into my fists. "Legs together."

I don't try to plead or resist. *If I show him how willing I am to take his punishment, his anger, he'll be able to forgive me. Max, please forgive me!*

I feel a little thump next to me and try to move my head to see. "No. Keep your face down." I stop moving. My hair becomes a cover around me. I breathe through the blanket, trying to calm myself. Waiting.

I hear the closet door open again. I jump when Max grabs my ankles, but he has a firm hold of them. *He's tying my feet to the bed?! With rope? Where did he get rope?* My mind circles. The rope burns a little as he tightens it.

"I'm not going to tie your hands, Lucy." *That's a relief.* "You'll have to keep them out of the way on your own." *That doesn't sound good.*

"If you move," He stops. His voice is deeper. The edge is sharper. He's trying not to growl his words, trying to keep his temper reigned in long enough to say what he needs to.

A bolt of fear shivers down my back and stabs my stomach. My mind dredges up the night he put me in the closet. His anger was barely in check then. He said he put me in there to keep me safe, away from his rage. *Tonight, he's not waiting. Tonight, he's not sheltering me from his wrath.*

"Don't move."

"...Please..." I'm too scared to stop myself. But I keep my face hidden, a muffled plea. I don't want to see the face that goes with his glass voice.

"Do you understand me, little girl?"

"Yes...yes, Sir." I hear him move to my left side. I can't hold in my fear. I lift my head a little, "Max! Please..." I cry and shake. "I'm sorry....please."

I hear a whoosh and feel the belt. A fire across the middle of my cheeks wraps around my hip. I scream, a high cry of pain and shock. He doesn't wait for my next plea. I don't know if he hit me two or three times in a row, a fire spreads from the same spot. In my mind, I'm a rabbit running for the bushes. But I keep my hold on the bed.

I can't catch my breath, Max hits me again. And again. And again.

My throat burns from screaming into the bed. My body is drenched and trembling. He pauses only long enough for me to catch a quick breath, my plea is torn with another searing crack of his anger. The belt rises and falls four more times.

Fire and ice. Heat peaks, spreads, pushes numbness aside. *Run, rabbit, run.*

But I stay. Eyes and fists balled. Tears soak tears. I lose count of the blows.

My cry doesn't stop. I pull it in and push it out. Air is a painful punishment. And Max doesn't stop.

He moves to the other side of the bed. Tick tick tick. I have only a moment before he starts again. A gulp of hot air, choking on tears and snot and hair and blanket.

The fresh angle sends shooting pain. Fire pain to skin yet touched by his anger. Ice pain to welts well whealed.

The bed moves with my convulsions. I don't know when Max finally stops. I keep the bed moving.

31 Him

I have to stop.

I have to stop.

Stop. Goddammit!

Stop!

But I feel my legs move. Around to the other side. I feel my arm lift. Belt in the air. I feel the impact with her. I watch her swollen cheeks dance under my belt. And I lift my arm again.

Lucy's cries fill me. I need them. I need her.

Finally. I stop.

But I watch. Her ass continues to shade red and purple. Her hips and thighs are crisscrossed with clear belt marks. The middle is bruises under bruises. Her body pushes up and down with sobs. Her head bobs uncontrollably, her mouth is wide open under her mass of hair. Finally, a deep sob out turns to shattered gulps for air and control.

I watch.

Lucy's arms are still stretched. Hands are still balled. Every muscle is still strained.

But she didn't move.

She took it.

And I'm hard.

I step back and drop the belt.

I watch my clothes fall to the floor. I watch my hands undo the ropes. I watch as I spread her legs.

I watch Lucy arch her back to me.

I stop.

32 Her

I don't hear Max.

I don't know where he is. Or if he'll start again.

Max beat me in silence. I cry a long moan at this. But I'm mute. My throat doesn't want to give any more voice to my pain.

I hear a thud and metallic clang on the floor. And panting.

Max is standing at the end of the bed? Watching me?

I feel a hard tug at my ankles and cry out. It's a harsh cracked sound.

He releases me.

I loosen my grip on the bed. Close my mouth against it. *It's over*?

Max opens me. And I arch to him.

Every inch of me is on fire. The pain fills the cracks in the icy numbness. But I arch to him.

Fill me with your forgiveness!

He stops.

I move my face to the side. A hot hoarse whisper, "Please...forgive me."

Max lands hard on the bed, legs pinned against my hips, rocking me against him. The heat of his ass and balls slaps against the heat of my ass and thighs. I cry out, no sound.

When the bed stills, he puts his hands gently on my ass. Heat sears us to be one.

He pulls me apart. The heat escapes for a moment, shoved back in with his first thrust.

He's brutal. Hard. Pounding.

And I meet him with each violent push into me. Arched for each one.

"You are mine."

"I am yours." Barely a crackle.

"You are mine."

No sound.

We come together. His choked words. Mine no sound.

I close my eyes. Max moves off gently. I pull my arms down to the side of my head.

"Don't move." *I don't think I could if I wanted to*. Every muscle burns. *My butt*...I run from focusing on this. *Let the numbness stay a little longer*.

I watch through my hair as he returns with cool towels. He places one across my butt. A shock waves tension through me again. I cry out, soundless.

He pushes my hair back and wipes my face with the other towel. "Blow." And Max holds the towel while I blow into it. He wipes me clean.

"I'm getting ice." And I watch as he walks away. I close my eyes when he's gone.

The towel wiping between my legs startles me awake. A crack in my voice is hardly the sound of a cry. He places a new towel on my butt, gently, and places a bag of ice on this, gently.

"Open your mouth." And I do, my eyes follow his fingers from a glass to my mouth. He places an ice cube on my tongue and my throat welcomes the relief. My heat melts it quickly.

I open my mouth for another. He places it for me.

"Close your eyes and sleep, baby." And I do.

My eyes shoot open at the pain. The ice falls to the side. It's dark, but the bathroom light is on.

I can see Max clearly. He moves quickly to take the ice away. He must have been awake, sitting next to me this whole time.

"Do you need the bathroom?"

I try to say yes, but my throat burns. I only nod.

He gets up and gently slides me towards him. He's gentle but my butt cries against movement. He rolls me to the side and I wince; my eyes squeeze shut. He picks me up and carries me to the bathroom. The light blinds me for a moment. I squeeze my eyes shut again, blocking the view of my swollen and bruised body.

Gently, he puts me down, my hands grip his arms. He braces me over the toilet. The humiliation is nothing to the relief, but returns to the forefront when he wipes me. I lean my forehead onto his cool shoulder. *Look at what has become of me.*

Max carries me back to the bed and gently places me on my left side. I stay curled up and he puts a pillow under my head and pulls the blanket over me.

Wiping my hair away, "I'm going to get you some juice." I watch him walk away.

I open my eyes to the sound of the glass on the nightstand. *I thought I'd kept them open.*

He holds the glass for me, holds my head for me. I cough on the juice against my throat, but this helps. He puts a pill in my mouth. "This will help you sleep, baby." And I do. I thankfully drift back to blackness quickly. *I don't want to think of what Max has done to me.*

I'm awake. *And alone.* I move slowly, testing where I still hurt. I pull my legs over the side of the bed and push myself up to stand.

Okay. Good. I'm standing. Now for moving.

Walking is painful. Light steps quake my butt. I can't tell where my butt and thighs meet or end. It's all just one giant thumping pain and little screaming pains jumping up and down. *But I'm moving.*

In the bathroom, I stare at the toilet. *Nope. Can't do it. Can't sit. Don't even want to try.*

I turn to the shower instead. I wait for the steam on the door. But with my head down, eyes not looking at my reflection. *Not ready to see myself yet.*

The warm water is a relief, my face and hands go up to the rainhead. I pee. *I don't care.*

I wash, gently, not putting my hands on my butt, keeping the water on my front. Small movements help.

The fluffy soft towel isn't soft enough, but I wrap myself in it anyway, over my head, around my body. *My cocoon.*

Deep breath. *Look. Just look and be done with it.*

I lower the towel and look at my face. *Puffy eyes, red nose. Good. No bruises this time.*

I turn a little. *Deep breath, just keep breathing.* I quickly lower the towel and gasp.

I'm a railroad of belt lines on my hips and thighs with an epicenter of purple. The side of my left breast is a big bruise. I can't look away. I turn more to see a different reflection. *Is that* my *butt? My legs?* The pain answers yes.

I pull the towel back up to my chin and stare into my eyes.

The pain is what I deserve. For my stupidity. My betrayal. I should've left last night when Rich showed up. I shouldn't have let him sit next to me. Drunk. I shouldn't have let him touch me. Drunk, leaning on me.

I should've had the strength to walk away. But I didn't want to upset Laura or Tracy. I didn't want to make a scene in front of Rosa.

I look into my eyes and try to remember what I thought last night. *Did I think I could get away with it?* Because Max wasn't supposed to be there. *Did I think that he wouldn't punish me as he promised if he found out?*

Max always keeps his promises. I knew the consequence. I had no idea how much anger he kept hidden inside. But I knew the consequences of pushing open that door. Pushing the limits of his forgiveness.

I shake, burying my face into my fists, holding the towel up, remembering Max's look of pure anger, right before he grabbed me. It all seemed to happen so fast. *But that look...I didn't know him.*

I remember what I thought when I turned away from the terrace...*that I had to get away from him.* That thought flew away quickly, but it shocked me.

And I pull my head up to see his face in reflection at the door now.

No anger. No expression. Just watching me.

I slowly drop the towel and let him see. I know Max has kept watch over me all night. He's seen. But I offer him myself now.

I try to speak, but have to swallow several times to get my voice to work, hoarse and sore. He just waits, quiet. "I'm sorry, Sir." He remains expressionless, blinking. "Thank you." I think this is what he's waiting for.

But Max stays at the door, his eyes slowly coming up from my butt to my eyes.

There's pain there now. His voice gravels over the words, "You're sorry? Look at what I did to you."

I shake my head, but stop when he moves closer. With his hand on my chin, he looks at my butt in the mirror. "I said I would do this. Didn't you believe me, little girl?"

"...Yes, Sir." His fingers under my chin forcing my head back make my throat strain even more to get the confession out.

"And still you defied me?"

"Yes, Sir." He lowers his hand and I lower my chin a little, swallowing.

"Then you got what you deserved." But he says this so quietly.

"Yes, Sir." I start my apology again, to try to explain, "I should've left when Ri..."

"Don't say his name to me." Anger flares in his eyes and I lower mine in submission. "If you know what's good for you, little girl, you'll never say that name again." I watch his stomach flutter with a deep breath. Shutting the door on his anger again, his voice returns to calm, "You should've obeyed me. You shouldn't have been anywhere near another man. And yes, you should've left."

"Yes, Sir."

"You'll be staying home for the next two weeks. And you won't be continuing your friendship with Tracy." I shoot my eyes up to him at this, no defiance, just questioning. "Laura told me that she invited that man last night." I only nod once, lowering my eyes again. *I didn't know that.* I thought it was a coincidence that Rich showed up. "I won't have my wife whoring around with a slut that thinks that's okay." His words stab me.

"Yes, Sir." He starts to turn away and I panic. "...Max?" He doesn't say anything, the pain in his face is replaced for a moment by concern though. "Do you...do you forgive me?"

He puts his hands on both sides of my head and kisses my forehead. "Of course, baby." He gently wraps his arms around me and I know he's looking at my butt again. I bury my face in his chest. I can feel his cock hardening under his boxers.

He gets hard seeing his marks on me. I get wet knowing this. I don't try to analyze it. It's just us.

When he tries to move away, I hold on tighter, kissing his chest. He gently pulls me away with a firm grip on my shoulders. "I can't. It'd hurt you too much."

"Please..." I try to push against his hands but the pain shoots from my butt and thighs. I wince a sharp breath in, out. I need to feel his forgiveness even if it will hurt.

He hesitates. A twisted grimaced grin appears before his mouth smashes mine. His hands find my tits, squeezing, travelling down, cupping my pussy. His palm is wet from me; a finger slides in easily, pressing hard against me. A moan is ripped from me, raw in my shredded throat.

"You want me?"

"Yes...please, yes!"

Max lowers his head to my neck, lips kissing my heartbeat, "I won't be gentle, Lucy."

"I know."

I clutch at his arms, nails digging in, wanting more. He turns me quickly to face the counter. I brace my hands and bend forward a little, on tip-toe, ignorant of the pain now. He enters me gently, deeply, watching my face in reflection. His body is cool against my ass.

I cry out when he grips my hips, but he doesn't let go, holding me in place. He pulls back almost to the tip. With a twisted grin, he rams into me, tearing a scream from deep in me. The pain shoots out in all directions. But he only pulls back for another thrust.

He watches me in the mirror. I try to catch my breath, speared on his cock, legs shaking, hands slipping on the counter. He slaps into me again. A moaning cry, an animal almost freed, but still painfully trapped, escapes me. Max fucks me slow and hard, keeping his eyes on my face. He watches the explosion of pain, the release of pleasure. He takes it all in and makes it his.

We don't last long. His thrusts speed us to our finish. I'm sobbing again, my orgasm, the pain, his forgiveness. All rolled into one. *What have I become?*

He turns me gently and holds me against his chest. My tears matt his hair down. I stop when I taste his sweat and my saltiness mixed. I want to cry on him more, to have him slap away all memory of my betrayal.

He gently pulls away and looks into my face, wiping my cheeks with his palms.

"You've been punished enough, baby. Time to get back in bed and rest more." *He always knows what I'm thinking.*

I meekly let him lead me to the bed and tuck me in again. He rubs my head until I drift off.

33 Him

"She's sleeping now, Laura. I'll tell her you called." I look at my watch, it's almost three in the afternoon. *I should get her up soon to eat something.*

"So...everything's okay between you guys...?"

"We're fine."

"You weren't fine last night." Laura sounds nervous.

I laugh at her understatement. "No, I was pissed as Hell last night. Another man's hand on my wife? What do you think?"

"But...Lucy's okay today? I'd really like to talk to her, Max..." *She's a sweet girl. Submissive at heart, whether she knows it or not.* I know Laura is the one friend that Lucy confides in, talks to about our marriage.

"Lucy's fine, Laura. She's resting after the spanking I gave her last night." I don't give her time to respond, her little intake of breath is enough of one. Lucy must not have told her that part. "And she won't be taking any calls or visits for the next two weeks either as a part of her punishment." I have a sudden thought. Tracy's been texting and calling her all morning too. I don't know why I didn't think of this before. "I'll be getting Lucy a new phone and number. She'll call you in two weeks."

"Oh...okay." Before I can hang up though, "Max?"

"Yeah?"

"Tell Lucy that I'm sorry...that I didn't help her more last night. She really tried to keep a distance from Rich, but he was drunk and just kept leaning over and grabbing all of us."

I know she's only trying to help, thinking she can explain it away; but hearing this only peaks my anger again. "Lucy knows that it was her own fault. She doesn't blame you. I'll let her know you called." And I hang up the phone.

And fuck me if Lucy's phone isn't vibrating again before I can put it down. *Unknown caller.* Instinct. I pick up.

"Hello."

"Oh...uh...Is Lucy there?"

"Hello, Rich." I keep my voice even. I lean back against the kitchen counter.

"Can I talk to Lucy?" He's trying to sound strong.

"No, Rich, you can't talk to *my* wife, *Mrs*. Traeger. You won't be talking to her again."

"I just want to apologize for being drunk...and to see if she's okay." He tries again to sound like he has balls.

"Another man checking on *my* wife? I don't think so. I think that it's in your best interest to forget that you even knew *my* wife."

"What's that supposed to mean? Are you threatening me?"

"No. I'm *promising* you that if you talk to my wife again, if you even get anywhere near her again, I will *break...your...fucking...arms.*" I don't raise my voice, just let the anger idle on low. I don't want to wake Lucy.

"You're fucking crazy! I could sue you, threatening me like this."

"I'm a good lawyer." I hang up and turn her phone off. *At least I don't have to track him down to settle that now.*

I walk back to the bedroom. Lucy is still sleeping, her body in a loose ball, the sheet only covering half her ass.

The sight of my anger on her body...the mess of bruises and welts...I feel my cock stiffen. I run my hands through my waves and breathe out quietly.

I know I'm a monster. To do that to her. To like *doing that to her. Hell, to get off doing that to her.*

It's not just her cries, her tears that turn me on. Watching over her last night, I realized that it was her willingness, her yielding to my anger. That she would stay on the bed, not moving, taking whatever I would do to her. That she thinks like I do...that she deserved to suffer for her disobedience. That she wouldn't be my good girl again without taking my punishment.

I'm a monster. And she loves me anyway. She surprised me with her eagerness though. I know I've made her wet with lighter spankings, slappings. But last night, this morning, in her pain...she wanted to please me. She said before that she craves my touch, tender or rough, she just craves me.

She's mine.

I've given up the fear of losing control. Even last night, I was in control. I hurt her this badly on purpose, no hesitation. But I was in control.

But last night, I gave up the fear that my anger could ever push her away. She'll take my anger and make it her pain.

She's mine.

34 Him

"Lucy! I'm home." She usually comes running, giggling and slaps my chest when I do my bad Cuban impersonation. "Lucy?"

I walk into the kitchen and drop off the pizza I picked up for us. I stop. The dishes from lunch are still sitting on the counter. I clench my jaw. *She better have a damn good reason for not getting this chore done before I'm home.* It's only been a few days since I had to spank her for talking back. *She won't be sitting for dinner.*

And I stop again. *She had a doctor's appointment this afternoon.* She's been extra tired the past few weeks and even though the EPT was negative yesterday, I made her the appointment. I've been stuck in client meetings all afternoon, so I haven't been able to check what the doctor said. I called earlier but figured Lucy was running around getting her chores done before the charity concert tonight.

I smile. *Being excited at the news of being pregnant would count as a damn good reason.*

I walk quickly into the hallway to the bedroom. Everything's right here. Laundry put away, bed made again. *She got through most of her list today at least.* I take off my coat and shoes and leave them by the bed. The bathroom light is on.

But she's not here, and she left the bathroom a mess. My anger is peaking again. *She's really pushing it.* I walk quickly down the hall to the den. *No Lucy.* Guest room. Bathroom. Terrace. *No Lucy.* I walk back to the kitchen and grab my phone off the counter. *No texts, no calls.*

Goddammit, little girl. Good news or not, you are getting an ass beating when you get home! Where the fuck are you? I dial her cell and Lucy's voice picks up right away.

"This is Lucy. Leave a message."

I hang up without leaving one. She'll see my call and know she's in trouble.

I check the voicemail on the home phone.

"Hi, guys. Just calling to see how you're feeling today, sweetie. And how your doctor's visit went...Fingers crossed!" Lizzie, her mom. She knows we've been trying for three months. Lucy talked to her yesterday.

"Hi, Max. Lucy. Give us a call when you're finished with your appointment today. We're thinking happy healthy thoughts for you, Lucy. Love you both!" My mom. I told her last night about the appointment.

"Hello. This message is for Lucy Traeger. This is Dr. Patel's office. You've missed your scheduled appointment with us today. Please call our office to reschedule at your earliest convenience. Per our office policy, you will be charged our late cancellation fee of $50 for this missed appointment. Thank you."

A cold steel rod raps around my stomach, stabbing my balls. *Lucy missed her appointment?*

"Hey, baby. Call me if you have news. I'm stuck in damn contract negotiations again, but I'll pick up. Oh...I'll grab a pizza for us before the concert. Wear your green dress. I love you, baby." My message. *She didn't listen to it. She didn't listen to any of these.*

"Hey, Luce. You haven't answered your texts, so I'm hoping it's because you and Max are celebrating...some good news maybe? Call me!" Laura.

I pick up the phone and dial Lucy again.

"...Leave a message." Her happy, sweet girl voice. The steel tightens.

"Lucy. You better call me right back if you know what's good for you, little girl." All my anger, my fear trembles into my message.

I text her the same.

I wait half a minute. No response. I call Laura first.

"Hey!" Laura's excitement loosens the steel a little.

"Hey, Laura. Is Lucy with you?" I try to sound controlled, not angry, not afraid. *Maybe she wanted to share her good news with her best friend...*

"What? No...I thought you were Lucy calling me back. I haven't heard from her since yesterday..."

I can't breathe. I can't speak. *Where the fuck is my wife*?!

"Max? Where's Lucy?"

"I...I don't know." My vision swims and I grab the counter. *Shit.*

In six months of marriage...I've never not known where she is.

"I have to check with a few more people. I'll call you back." I hang up before she can say anything more.

I go to the den and start up my computer, trying to slow my breathing while waiting. I don't wait well. *Finally.* I start up the monitoring app I installed on Lucy's phone.

No messages or calls answered today. My message stares back at me. *Not even picked up. Nothing is picked up.*

The GPS shows the phone is stopped near her doctor's office.

But she missed her appointment.

What the fuck are you doing, little girl?!

I walk back to the bedroom. Put my shoes back on. Grab my coat.

In the kitchen I grab my wallet and keys. I text Jeff to meet me downstairs. I'll get in a cab if he isn't here first.

I dial, "Jake. No. Stop....I need your help." He listens as I give him directions.

"She's not here, Max. There's nobody here." The darkened office buildings sentinel over me, crushing my heart, pinning the steel rod into me more.

I try Lucy's cell again, no answer. No whistle ringtone. I've tried up and down the street. "She's got to be here, Jeff." I hear the weakness. I hear the anger. Fear. Pain.

I sent Jake back to the apartment in case she showed up there. He hasn't heard anything.

Jeff stops in front of a garbage bin.

"It's time to call the police, Max." His voice is cold. Jeff puts his hand up to stop me from reaching into the bin. Halfway down, on a pile of papers and food, the blue light of Lucy's phone is sitting on top of her purse. He looks at me, but I'm not seeing him through the tunnel of darkness. "Don't touch anything. I'll call a friend on the force." He turns away and I don't hear him, frozen in place.

Max and Lucy finish their story with completely different,

alternative endings, *True Control* 4.1 & 4.2

1 Him

"Mr. Traeger, we just need to go over this one more time." The short detective is taking a seat at my table across from me. I didn't tell him he could. I've given up control of my apartment, my car, my office.

The other detectives are standing in a group near my terrace doors, staying out of the way of the people working around my living room. They've already finished with the other rooms. I haven't talked to this detective yet. He just stood in the background up until now.

With my head in my hands still, I growl, "I've been over this and over this." I look up, my bloodshot eyes bouncing around the room full of cops. "When are you people going to tell *me* something?!" Jeff puts his hand on my shoulder to try to calm me, but this only angers me more. I stand up quickly and go to the kitchen.

Jake is leaning against the counter. He shakes his head and hands me a small scotch. I shouldn't be drinking, not now, but I need to calm my nerves.

Jeff comes in and says quietly, "Max, you need to cooperate. I know this is frustrating, but this is how it works. This *is* how we'll find Lucy." *I know he's right*. He got the ball moving fast on this, calling in favors from his cop days. I take another gulp and put the glass down, a little calmer. I walk back to the dining table and sit down.

"Max!" Dad pushes past two cops by the door and rushes to me. I smile slightly, seeing his look of shock and anger, I know it mirrors my own. My brother's been trying to stay calm and neutral for my sake, but Dad isn't one to hide his feelings behind a mask.

"Where's Mom?"

"Jake said it was a zoo here. I thought it'd be best if she comes later. When we get this place cleared out."

"Good." I turn to the detective again. Taking a deep breath, "Where do you want me to start?"

"You said the last time you saw or spoke to your wife was when you left after lunch," he refers to his notes, "about 1:00?"

"Yes. We had lunch together here. Lucy had an appointment with her doctor at 2:00. Jeff drove me to my client meetings in the afternoon." I say this last part through gritted teeth. I still blame myself for not having Jeff drive her. I had too many appointments all over town today; I needed him to keep me on schedule.

"Sorry to interrupt, Det. Killaney. We have everything we need here." The detective nods to the uniformed cops and watches as most of the people leave my apartment. *It's a mess of dust and prints and tossed shit everywhere*. They've searched every inch of the apartment looking for any sign of a struggle or hint where Lucy could be. I didn't think they'd find anything here, but I let them loose to do what they needed to do. *My car and office must look the same.*

"And that was with her OB/GYN doctor," again back to the notes, "Dr. Patel?"

"Yes. Her office left a message that Lucy missed the appointment." I'm starting to go numb giving these details again. *It's either go numb or go ballistic.*

"I got three."

"What?" Through my numbness, I frown at him.

"Three kids. Three boys. Have you been trying long?"

"No." I don't want to answer questions about this. It's too painful to think about Lucy missing and possibly pregnant too.

The detective leans in a little to look at my face more closely. "Ya know it takes some couples a long time to get pregnant. My wife and I were lucky; well, if you call having three boys in less than four years lucky."

I know he's pushing me, to get me out of my numbness, but I'm drained. Dad isn't, he reacts quickly. "Detective, can I ask what the hell that has to do with anything? Or how that helps find my daughter-in-law?"

The detective looks up slowly at my dad and I follow his eyes up too. Dad has his stern "lawyer pushing a client to do what he says look" that I've seen so often. I can see Jake standing with Jeff in the background, both tense. "Sir. Can I get your name for the record?"

"Ronald Traeger. Now answer my question, Detective."

"I'm trying to help your son to remember as much detail as he can." He looks at me, his eyes narrowing, taking in my slumped shoulders and broken state. "I think he's at his limit though in answering questions tonight."

"No. I want to get through this. Go on. Ask what you need to." I'm still numb though. Killaney raises his eyebrows, but goes back to his notepad.

"So when you didn't hear from your wife this afternoon, you tracked her phone?"

"No. I assumed Lucy was busy with her chores. I tracked her phone when I got home and found she wasn't here and wasn't answering my calls or texts."

He picks up the baggie that has the list of chores I'd left for Lucy this morning. "And this is your handwriting; this is a list of *chores* for your wife?"

"Yes."

"And you do this, leave a similar list, each morning?" I can see yesterday's list in a ball in another bag. They must've pulled it from the trash.

"Yes." I can feel Dad tensing behind me, his hand is on the back of my chair.

Det. Killaney continues holding the bag, but changes directions in questions, "But you didn't just track the GPS, you were able to check her calls and messages too?"

"Yes. I have an app that allows me to check her calls, texts, voicemail and GPS."

"And you often check these things...your wife's calls and messages?" He says this quietly, looking down at his notes before bringing his eyes to stare into mine, sizing me up again.

"Not often."

"What? Every day, every other day, once a week...?"

"Usually only if she leaves the house."

"So, what happens if Lucy doesn't get through her chores?" He's appraising me again.

I knew this would come up. So far, it hadn't, but this must be the 'bad cop.'

Dad butts in, "I think Max does need a break, Detective."

I don't take my eyes off Killaney. "Dad. It's fine. I need them to get through eliminating me as a suspect as quickly as possible to focus on what happened to Lucy."

"Why would I think you're a suspect, Max?" Killaney's stare is alert again, but he keeps his body purposefully relaxed.

"Isn't the husband always the first one?"

He laughs, "Usually. But you seem awfully calm about that..."

I only shrug. Jeff had talked me through all this on the drive back to my apartment and while waiting for everyone to show up. Eventually, all the details of my marriage with Lucy will come to light if the investigation goes on. *God. If my Lucy isn't found.*

I lower my head at this thought. *My Lucy. Where are you, little girl?*

"So…what happens?" I look dumbly up at him, so he spells it out for me, "What happens if your wife doesn't finish the chores you've given her, Max?"

I answer calmly, from a tunnel in my head, "It depends on the chore, on her excuse."

He picks up the list and reads, "Run two miles in under thirty-five minutes. What if she didn't get this one done?"

"I crossed it off the list. Lucy wasn't feeling well this morning again."

"Hmmm…morning sickness or something else?"

I narrow my eyes again, even in my haze I don't like discussing this. "I don't know."

"So…what about this one; it's not crossed off." He points towards the bottom of the list. "What if Lucy didn't get your suit from the dry cleaners, Max? What would happen?"

"She didn't."

"What?"

"She didn't get to most of those chores today. The dry cleaning would've been hanging in the front of the closet if she had."

"And when you got home, you checked?"

"Not right away. I checked when Jeff and I got back here. While we waited."

"Hmmm…and what were you going to do if Lucy walked in the door while you were waiting…with all these chores undone?" He's quiet, calm, like we're discussing the weather instead of my missing wife.

Dad clears his throat. "I think that's enough questions, son."

"I would've punished her."

True Control 4.2 is the alternative ending.